Magic Mantras

MAGIC MANTRAS

FOR *young adults*

TO ACHIEVE SUCCESS IN LIFE

Laxmi Dhaul

Illustrations by
Vinayak Pendurkar

NIYOGI
BOOKS

Published by
NIYOGI BOOKS
D-78, Okhla Industrial Area, Phase-I
New Delhi-110 020, INDIA
Tel: 91-11-26816301, 49327000
Fax: 91-11-26810483, 26813830
email: niyogibooks@gmail.com
website: www.niyogibooksindia.com

Illustrations: Vinayak Pendurkar

Editor: Mohua Mitra/Niyogi Books
Cover design: Write Media
Layout: Sarojini Gosain/Niyogi Books

ISBN: 978-93-83098-20-0
Publication: 2014

Printed at: Niyogi Offset Pvt. Ltd., New Delhi, India

'To finish the moment, to find the journey's end in every step of the road, to live the greatest number of good hours, is wisdom.'

—Ralph Waldo Emerson

To
my children Mikhail, Karan and Veda
who have taught me the greatest lessons in life

The Magic Mantras

DREAM
Dream
Goal 4
Goal 3
Goal 2
MAP

Introduction

You are young, confident and feel ready to make your mark in the world. Everything you've ever wanted is very close–all you have to do is reach out and take it! But as you extend your hand, you realise it isn't as easy as it seems and what was once "oh so close" suddenly seems far away! Life seems to have pulled the rug from under your feet! Then what do you do? You try harder and harder, and the more you try the further your dream seems to slip away! And when you *stop* trying, your dream just fades into the distance!

So what CAN you do? You can close your eyes and call on your Magic Mantras.

What is a mantra? Those familiar with Sanskrit texts will recall that a mantra is a stanza composed of sacred words, which when repeated over and over give tremendous strength. That's exactly what these Magic Mantras are for; to help you discover the tremendous strength that is already inside you.

Why do we need these Magic Mantras?

Adolescence is a transitional phase. It is a confusing, rebellious, beautiful, miserable, exciting phase of constant change. A phase in which you may have to shed beliefs you have unquestioningly clung on to till now; and it's the period when people suddenly start looking at you differently. It is the stage where you would like to be treated differently and take charge of your own life! So you find yourself oscillating between adulthood, and the responsibility that accompanies it; and childhood with all its carefree irresponsibility. During this stage, you may suddenly find your perception of your parents changing drastically, your family fortunes rising or dwindling suddenly, and strange new relationships are rushing into your life without warning, dragging complex emotions with them. When this happens, don't panic, just relax, this is completely normal! With these Magic Mantras, you'll learn to be positive and enjoy the rollercoaster you're on!

During your teenage years, you are gradually developing a new personality. It's a bit like fine-tuning a radio. In order to get the best clarity, you have to find the right frequency. Similarly, the change going on within you may not be visible externally and may just require you to keep making some minor 'frequency' changes, till your personality is just perfectly *you*! This is certainly a confusing time, and it's important to remember one thing … *you must be patient with yourself.* Right now, you need to *build,* not *beat,* yourself up! Take a deep breath, and *believe in yourself.* The mantras in this book will help you to understand and cope with the changes you are going through, and at the same time to unleash the vast potentials that lie within you.

Adolescence is also the stage in life when a lot of important questions need to be answered. What should I study? Where should I live? What should my career be? Should I trust this person? These questions may seem overwhelming but it's comforting to know that all of them ultimately lead you to *finding yourself*. You may ask if these Magic Mantras will help you find your answers over the next few years, and the answer is YES. These Magic Mantras will guide you to discover who you really are and what you really want. Then it will help you go out and achieve your dreams!

People will listen to your ideas, you will get admission into the university of your choice, the girl/boy you are in love with will accept you as you are, you will get everything you want out of life … but if, and *only* if, you believe in yourself. There are tomes of written material available about positive thinking and how to live better lives: books that will help you advance spiritually, mentally, socially, and physically. This book is your own personal guide–simply talking straight to you, the way a friend would.

I sincerely hope these Magic Mantras will help you on your journey of life; please believe that you have everything within you to make this journey truly remarkable … All the best!

Laxmi Dhaul
September 2013

A friend is someone who knows the words to the song in your heart and can sing it back to you when you have forgotten the words.

—Bernard Meltzer (1916-1998)

Radio host in the United States for several decades. Meltzer's show provided counsel on a wide range of quandaries

Magic Mantra One

I BELIEVE IN MYSELF

Magic Mantra One

I believe in myself

Tapping and unlocking your inner potential

Whether you think you can, or think you can't ... either way you're right.

—Henry Ford
American industrialist,
the founder of the Ford Motor Company.

The elephant's pole

In a circus one fine morning, a baby elephant was born. This baby elephant was so lively and curious about all things around him that the circus ringmaster decided to tie him to a pole so that he wouldn't be able to run away. And so the baby elephant was shackled to an iron chain around a pole, and try and tug as he might, he just couldn't break free! He tried every day, and the days flowed into weeks ... till he realised the pole was much bigger and stronger than he was. So, he gave up.

This baby elephant grew into a big, towering elephant, mighty and strong, and much more powerful than the pole he was tied to. But, he remained bound to his little pole! He clung to his childhood belief that he was weaker than the measly pole that anchored him. He never tried his strength against the pole or to break free, because he clung to the memory of his first failure!

Then one fine morning, a gorgeous butterfly came up to him and he reached out to touch its wings. Lost in its fluttering colours, he forgot about the chain shackling his foot to the pole and jumped wildly towards the butterfly ... Lo behold, the pole bent, the chain snapped, and he was free! The elephant was stunned; he himself had no idea he had so much strength in him! And he realised he had finally broken free of his greatest limitation ... the limitation created by his own mind and the mental patterns established when he was young, when in fact, the situation was quite different!

Seize the opportunity

We are often exactly like that baby elephant! If we are told something repeatedly as children, we accept them as facts, and these 'facts' soon become our reality! We need to review our thoughts and let go of the outdated beliefs – no more relevant – that we held as children. For example, 'Don't talk to strangers' may be an important instruction for a child, but it won't take you far as a marketing professional! If as a child you were compared unfavourably to your sibling or a family friend's child, it's most likely that you developed the feeling that you were not talented enough and that you should hold yourself back forever! You've got to move past that and try your hand at whatever you wish! You have to believe in yourself, rather than live in the shadow of words said to you ages ago. Besides, does it even matter if years ago someone was supposedly better than you? In this age of opportunity and innovation, the most unlikely talents spring forth and are hailed in the world as truly amazing.

Did you know that Bill Gates dropped out of Harvard to follow his dream of setting up his own company? Microsoft was born in his **garage** soon after he dropped out!

Stephen Hawking is an internationally renowned physicist who has made groundbreaking contributions to the study of the cosmos and quantum gravity. His books on popular science include the revolutionary bestseller *A Brief History of Time.* However, when Hawking was in school, he was not considered bright by many of his classmates!

According to the *Guinness Book of World Records,* Agatha Christie is the best-selling novelist of all time. She has sold roughly 4 billion copies of her sixty-six books, translated into more than a 100 languages! It's amazing to know that this author suffered from dysgraphia, a disorder that made it difficult for her to remember spellings or write legibly, so that she needed to dictate all her books to a typist. But that did not stop her from following her passion to write novels!

And Beethoven, one of the most famous and influential music composers of all time, was struck by a terrible tragedy at a very young age. When he was just twenty years old, his **hearing began to deteriorate!** But he continued to conduct, compose and perform music even after he became **completely deaf**!

All these achievers overcame major handicaps to become truly great. Take inspiration from them, and at least try to overcome childhood jibes that may not even be true!

Conquer your dreams

'It is not the mountain we conquer but ourselves.'

—Edmund Hillary
one of the first two climbers
to reach the summit of Mount Everest.

Learn to push your own boundaries; great things are achieved only by those who *try*. Work at overcoming your own failings, **the road may be difficult but the rewards are immense.**

Often, we have a strange fear of discovering the potential hidden inside us. Nelson Mandela himself said, 'Our deepest fear is that we are powerful beyond measure.' We fear the path to success will be difficult and require sacrifice, we see failure lurking on the side-walk, we fear what people will think and what people will say ... but we forget one important thing ... that once we push and find our inner potential, we will lead happier lives!

Grab that happier life for yourself, do not let fear paralyse you and keep you away from your dreams!

Wayne Gretzky, former professional ice-hockey player and head coach, is generally regarded as the best player in the history of the National Hockey League. He said, 'You miss 100 per cent of the shots you don't take!'

Do not let the fear of missing a shot keep you out of the game!

Most of the problems we see are in our own minds, and it is up to us to rise above them. Ignore whatever you perceive as your limitations, and watch them crumble to dust!

'Aerodynamically, the bumblebee shouldn't be able to fly, but the bumblebee doesn't know that so it goes on flying anyway!'

—Mary Kay Ash
famous American business entrepreneur who
founded the renowned cosmetic company
Mary Kay Cosmetics.

Believe to achieve

You may have heard of this interesting little concept called the 'placebo effect.' A placebo is a non-chemical sugar tablet, which is given to patients by drug testing companies. Chemically, these tablets have no medicinal properties but the patients don't know that, and take them as medicines. The surprising result is, very often, patients actually recover after taking those sugar tablets ... **simply because they believe they will!** Sometimes it is just the belief that we will be fine that actually makes us feel better! Never underestimate the power of the mind over the body and circumstances. Believe in yourself, and watch what heights you suddenly can reach.

'Confidence comes not from always being right but from not fearing to be wrong.'

—Peter T. McIntyre
well-known Second World War artist and writer
from New Zealand, initially achieved popularity as
a freelance commercial artist in NewZealand, UK,
USA and Australia; received the OBE.

Listen to your heart

Many of you will pass through this teenage period and remember it as the best time of your life. However, this is also the period when you will have to make important choices and take decisions that will have major repercussions in your life. The responsibility is great and maybe, intimidating. But decisions have to be taken and careers need to be carved out. People will always give you conflicting opinions; the key to success is to figure out what YOU want to do, check if that is realistically possible, be genuinely prepared to put your heart and soul into achieving your dreams, and then … simply take a deep breath and jump right in. Just Do It.

In the words of basketball super-star Michael Jordan – *'You have to expect things of yourself before you can do them.'*

Mozart: the child prodigy

Here's the inspiring story of Mozart, the famous composer, who wrote absolutely brilliant music as a child simply because he didn't let anyone stop him!

Mozart began composing at the age of five. As a child, he would sit by his elder sister while she learnt the piano, watching her intently and absorbing all he could. His father was stunned when the five-year-old Mozart handed him an ink-stained original composition! Shouldn't he have told his son that five-year-olds couldn't possibly compose music?

The six-year-old Mozart toured extensively, performing for

emperors and kings. Blissfully ignoring what society said he was capable or incapable of doing, Mozart wrote his first three symphonies by the age of eight! When he was twelve he wrote his first opera, and by the time he was a teenager, he had mastered the piano, violin, and the harpsichord! Unheard of, for how could someone so young understand the beauty of these instruments!

Mozart heard the music within him and he went for it, he did not wait till society said he was the right age to write music, or that he was old enough to appreciate symphonies. He just went ahead and did it, and by the young age of twenty-six, Mozart had composed 415 brilliant pieces of music! Mozart was a genius, but do not laugh away the idea that you may be special in your own way too. Mark Twain said, '*Thousands of geniuses live and die undiscovered—either by themselves or by others!*' Don't be afraid to discover yourself, you may be surprised by what you come up with!

So, if you have a wonderful idea for a novel bursting forth from your fingers, go ahead and write it, **now**. If you have a great new concept for a machine, go ahead and create it, **now**. If you've always dreamt of holding a photography exhibition, click those pictures and send them out, **now**. You are the perfect age **right now**! Do not wait for society to tell you it is time to follow your dreams. Seize the day ... and you will live a richer, happier, more extraordinary life.

> *'What lies behind us and what lies before us are tiny matters compared to what lies within us.'*
>
> —Henry S. Haskins, (1875–1957)
> stockbroker and man of letters. His aphorisms were
> edited and published anonymously in 1940.

Magic Mantra Two

I AM NOT LIMITED BY OTHER PEOPLE'S PERCEPTION OF ME

Magic Mantra Two

I am not limited by other people's perception of me

Understanding and accepting different views; balancing your self-esteem

Don't live DOWN those expectations. Go out there and do something remarkable!

—Wendy Wasserstein
American playwright and Professor-at-Large at Cornell University. Winner of Pulitzer Prize for Drama for *The Heidi Chronicles.*

The Muddled Eagle

An eagle's egg was once put into a nest of prairie chickens. The eaglet hatched with the brood of chicks and grew up with them. All its life, the changeling eagle, thinking it was a prairie chicken, did what all the other prairie chickens did. It scratched in the dirt for seeds and insects to eat. It clucked and cackled noisily. And it flew in a brief thrashing of wings and flurry of feathers no more than a few feet off the ground. After all, that's how prairie chickens were supposed to fly!

Years passed, and the changeling eagle grew bigger and stronger. One day, it saw a magnificent bird soaring high above in the cloudless sky. Hanging with graceful majesty on the powerful wind currents, it rose with scarcely a beat of its strong golden wings.

'What a beautiful bird! exclaimed the changeling eagle. 'What is it?' the eagle asked its neighbour—a prairie chicken.

'That's an eagle—chief of the birds,' the neighbour clucked. 'But don't give it a second thought. You could never be like him.' The changeling eagle looked up at the mighty eagle and sighed, resolving to put the thought out of his mind. After all, how could he, a mere chicken, aspire to be something so breathtaking?

But try as he might, the changeling eagle couldn't get the image of that powerful soaring bird out of his mind. So one day, he sneaked off to the topmost branch of the tree and looked down. The ground seemed scary and far away, and the little eagle almost stumbled back into the safe hollow of the tree. But a voice whispered to him from

deep down inside, and in his mind's eye, he saw the flash of his golden wings soaring far above to heights he would never have dared, and, with a thrill, he knew that with all his heart he wanted to fly like that. So taking a deep breath, he leapt into the cold air.

Air-borne, he felt the wind whip his weak wings and bring him downt ... he began to thrash his wings but could not stop his sharp spiralling descent. As the ground loomed crazily closer and closer he felt a sudden surge of current, like magic beneath his wings, that lifted him off easily. Soon he was flying, actually flying, soaring across the sky ... like the true eagle he was!

Very often we limit ourselves to the image that **other people have of us**. We believe we will fail, because others have told us we will. We stay within our comfort zones, because we think others will laugh at us if we venture out and make fools of ourselves. We even pursue popular careers, because that is what is considered 'right' or 'safe' for us; not realising that our actual abilities and talents lie elsewhere.

You need to realise that if you are to rise above another's perception of you and become truly great, you must first **see yourself as worthy of greatness**.

> *'Pay no attention to what the critics say. A statue has never been erected in honour of a critic!'*
>
> —Jean Sibelius
> the most noted symphonic composer of
> Scandinavia; identified with the
> Finnish nationalist movement.

Good Impressions

Come in!
Ah yes, what were you saying..yes, international conference..
Synergy!
Deadline! Budget!
Vertical Integration!
Confident he had made a smashing impression..
So what have you come for?
Sir, I'm just here to repair your telephone!
PHONE REPAIRS

Pretension and assumption are not cool!

Just like the executive of the above story, why do we feel this constant pressure to pretend for other people? Is it because we think we aren't good enough, so we're afraid of rejection, or afraid of being different? We often go out of our way and out of our minds, to make a good impression, either on someone we have a crush on, or on the 'cool crowd' in school, or even on people we will perhaps never see again.

It's important to be aware of one fact here–*no one is thinking about you as much as you worry they are, because … everyone is busy worrying about the exact same thing themselves!* You may now realise an important fact … a change in attitude and the way you perceive others can make you feel so relieved!

> *'Be who you are and say what you feel, because those who mind don't matter and those who matter don't mind.'*
>
> —Dr Seuss (Theodor Seuss Geisel)
> American poet, children's author, cartoonist and book publisher, best known for his books *The Cat in the Hat* and *Green Eggs and Ham.*

Perception is a funny power … it can change your attitude, your confidence, and even your relationship with someone. It's equally important to remember that perception is a two-way street; if you do not want to be judged and pigeon-holed by others, you should refrain from passing harsh judgement yourself!

Once I was on my way to a dentist's appointment, armed with the latest *Filmfare* magazine to pass the waiting time. While I waited, a young college girl sat next to me and to my horror, nonchalantly picked up my *Filmfare* and started flipping through it! I began to seethe, 'How dare she take my magazine without even asking? Really, how rude!' I spent a whole hour there, furious and fermenting, condemning the younger generation and its lack of manners. Even while my tooth was getting filled, I had hot rage roiling in my mind. I stepped out of the dentist's room, still thoroughly stirred up, and opened my purse to pay his fees. It was only then that I saw the magazine I had purchased lying there inside! It had been in my purse all along! I was so relieved that I had held my tongue and saved myself the embarrassment of being rude to that young girl! But I had already wasted a good hour in irritation and indignation, for no reason whatsoever!

Our perceptions of incidents are often incomplete, inaccurate, and often entirely wrong! Simply understanding the other person's perception can solve most of our problems!

This is especially true of a lot of relationships. Maybe you look at your father and feel that he is totally out of date with what you perceive is the trend of life; or maybe **your** perception of life has changed. On the other hand, it may be that he still looks at you like you're a spoilt brat and hasn't realised that you've become a young, sensitive, and intelligent young person. So, maybe … if you first prove that you **are** responsible, you can solve the friction between you and your father!

If you expect to be understood by others, you must try to understand others first. Understanding someone's beliefs, practices, or habits doesn't mean that you have to share their opinions. Learn to respect other people's opinions without automatically assuming that they are wrong just because they are different. It is a very human weakness to judge, criticise and even make fun of people whose thoughts and actions we don't understand. On the other hand, we hope for ourselves that the world will accept and praise our weaknesses and strengths, respectively. We hope to find appreciative friends who are happy and at peace with what we are–with our natural character traits. Be that friend first **yourself**.

The greedy king's fan

There was once a king who had *everything*; there was nothing he did not possess. Every morning, when he looked down from his castle at the bustling marketplace, he noted with great satisfaction that he had everything there; he had *ALL* the material possessions a man could ever want. This made his heart brim over with glee; he thought he must truly be the most powerful man in the world!

One morning, he was peering down his tower to satisfy his materialistic soul and got a rude shock instead! At the very centre of the market place was a merchant selling the most gorgeous fans he had ever seen! Colours, intricately carved handles, feather-light papers ... they were breathtaking! The king was filled with a burning longing–he simply had to possess those wonderful fans! So he ordered his soldiers to bring the merchant to his court immediately.

Soon the merchant was bowing humbly before the king. 'I would like to buy your fans!' the king said, and the merchant eagerly offered him his wares.

'Not these,' the king snapped. 'Everyone has already bought fans like these. Now I want something special and unique, something no-one else has!' he demanded.

Now the merchant was a shrewd trader who had heard of the king's passion for unique objects. So, he thought quickly and said in a hushed, mysterious voice, 'Ah, Your Majesty, I have just the fan for you … unique and special!' He reached into the deep recesses of his bundle and gently removed an old, dusty, folded fan. 'This is my most expensive fan,' he said, holding it up reverently 'because of its unique … ah … properties.'

'I want it!' the king said immediately and handed the merchant a huge bag of gold! The courtiers were shocked, a whole bag of gold in exchange for an old fan! But the king was delighted with his new purchase; the merchant handed the fan over to the king, bowed low, and left the royal court.

The next morning, the king decided to try out his wondrous new fan and ordered his servants to fan him with it. But the minute his servant opened the fan and shook it, it crumbled into a million pieces! There was a deathly silence in the court. The king then hollered at his soldiers to bring the merchant back!

His soldiers found the merchant, and brought him to the furious king. The merchant begged to be given a chance to explain why the fan broke so quickly.

'The fan is not of inferior quality, Sire!' he said. 'I had told you the fan had unique properties, and instructions on how to use it are engraved on the handle! Your servants did not read the instructions and used the fan in the wrong way. That's why it broke!'

'What is so different about this fan? What instructions?' growled the king, peering at the handle; 'If you are telling the truth, then I will forgive you and you can keep the bag of gold!'

'Yes, your Majesty,' the merchant replied, pointing at the instructions engraved on the handle. 'See, the instructions are – "To get wind from this fan, you need to hold the fan steady and shake your head in front of it!" I told you it was truly unique!'

The king was angry but stumped. It truly was a different fan, he couldn't argue with that! He wished he had clarified what was so unique about the fan before paying a whole bag of gold for it! He wished he had read the instructions before using and ruining his expensive fan!

So, the king had to let the clever merchant go, all because he was too foolish to clarify the merchant's intentional miscommunication!

This story may seem quite funny but it shows how what is actually perceived by one person may be very different from what other people *in the same place* see! The fan maker played on the ignorance, vanity, laziness, and misperception of the king and his royal durbar to his own advantage!

It all begins with you

This story reminds me of the time I landed in Vietnam

without a visa. My travel agent had assured me that I would get my visa on arriving at the airport there, so I had simply boarded the plane and reached! When I landed, however, Vietnamese officials told me that I needed to show them a clearance form issued by the consulate in India, on the basis of which they would give me my visa! I had no such form, and argued that my travel agent had simply told me that I would get my visa on arriving there; she had not mentioned anything about a clearance form! I was bluntly told that the rules were clear—if I did not have the clearance form they could not issue my visa.

I waited in a hot, airless arrival hall for over five hours while the mess was being resolved, and wished throughout that I had taken the five minutes needed to read the rules and instructions, and not relied blindly on my travel agent's casual statement! I finally emerged from this frustrating incident having learnt an invaluable lesson … to read instructions and be clear, because misperceptions can really land you in a mess!

All your perceptions together colour your whole outlook on life. They create your **attitude**. Your perceptions can make you gloomy or active, irritated or peaceful, jealous or confident. This is truly an empowering thought, because it means that only YOU are responsible for your own happiness and peace of mind, and that YOU can make your life miserable or joyous!

Yes, so it really does all begin … with you!

The whole world stinks!

One Sunday afternoon, a cranky old grandfather was visiting his family. As he lay down to take a nap, his grandson decided to have some fun by putting a particularly smelly slice of Limburger cheese on his grandfather's moustache. Soon, the grandpa awoke with a snort and charged out of the bedroom grumbling, 'This room stinks!' Through the house he went, finding every room reeking of the same stench. Desperately, he made his way outside, only to declare, 'The whole world stinks!'

That's exactly what happens when you fill your mind with negativity! Everything you experience and everybody you encounter will carry the scent you hold in your own mind. So make sure your mind is infused with fresh, positive thoughts that will draw people to you with their warmth and optimism!

Perception can even help you tackle problems. Instead of looking at difficulties as obstacles, see them as challenges, as opportunities to shine, or simply as opportunities to *learn*!

> *'Unless you try to do something beyond what you have already mastered, you will never grow.'*
>
> —Ralph Waldo Emerson
> nineteenth century American journalist, poet, essayist and philosopher of the Transcendentalist school.

The shoeless village

Here's a fun story about a shoe-salesman who once walked straight into his worst nightmare, and how he coped with it.

Once upon a time, there was a travelling salesman who sold every kind of shoe—leather, canvas, cloth, felt, rubber, and even plastic! His stock had every type of shoe your heart could desire, whether you wanted a fantastic design to adorn your feet, or a rugged sole to climb mountains in! This travelling salesman was very popular. People from all over the country used to beg him to customise and order shoes especially made for them.

One day, this salesman journeyed far into the interiors of the country and stood at the border of a strange village he had never come to before. He hiked his bag of wares up, entered the village, and was stunned! Not one person in the entire village wore shoes! Everyone was walking around barefoot, as happy as they could be!

The salesman was horrified; he had made a terrible mistake coming here! How would he sell his shoes to people who did not even know what shoes were?

As he walked slowly through the strange shoeless village, his heart sank lower and lower. No one, not even the chief of the village wore shoes! So the salesman lay down

his weary load and sighed bitterly. 'Coming here was a terrible mistake,' he thought miserably to himself. 'I'll leave tomorrow at dawn.' So he paid for a room at a lodge and fell into bed, exhausted and depressed.

That night, he had the strangest dream … he dreamt he was trying to pour a jug of water into two glasses. One glass was already half full and the water overflowed and sloshed over when he poured in water from the jug. The other glass was empty, and took in nearly all the water from the jug.

The salesman suddenly woke up, his heart beating wildly! He knew what he had to do! He sat up all night planning a grand opening for his shop!

The next morning, instead of packing up, he spread out all his wares on the ground and began to yell enthusiastically about the beauty, the sturdiness and the simple elegance of his shoes! He hollered about their colours, their utility, and their amazing designs! And soon, a curious crowd had gathered around the shop, and the salesman began doing brisk business!

The crowd grew larger and larger as the day progressed. It seemed *everyone* in the village wanted to own a unique pair of shoes!

Finally, as the sun set, the tired but happy salesman closed his shop. He had sold more shoes in one day than he had in the entire past week!

The salesman's dream had given him the key to unlocking great potential ... the potential of an undiscovered market!

It was when he stopped looking at the shoeless village as a problem, and started looking at it as a terrific opportunity just waiting to be explored, that he emerged as a real winner! That's what simply changing your perception can do for you!

'Where the loser saw barriers, the winner saw hurdles.'

—Robert Brault

veteran freelance American writer.

Magic Mantra Three

I AM THE PRODUCT OF MY CHOICES AND HAPPINESS BEGINS IN ME

Magic Mantra Three

I am the product of my choices and happiness begins in me

Being responsible and taking charge of your life

> *Destiny is not a matter of chance, it is a matter of CHOICE; it is not a thing to be waited for, it is a thing to be achieved.*
>
> —William Jennings Bryan (1860-1925) leading American politician from the 1890s till 1925. Dominant force in the populist wing of the Democratic Party.

Life is all about choices. Each choice leads to a consequence, which means we create our own possibilities ... and pitfalls! We are constantly making decisions; and have to learn to be careful and make sure they're **responsible** decisions. Acting in a responsible manner makes our lives better and more fulfilling. If we act irresponsibly, we will have to bear the consequences.

You are responsible for what happens to you!

Once you accept that, you'll realise how important your choices actually are. So how do you make sure you make the right choices? How do you know if the choices you have already made were the right ones? Well, it's a matter of trial and error; but the general guideline is simple—just follow your heart and do what sounds right to YOU.

Alexandra Stoddard writes in her book *Making Choices*—'You have to be really tough-minded to make choices. The great mystery about choice is that because you will NEVER be able to please everyone, nor even be understood by them, the only hope for you is to feel content about what you decide to do.' So, do what you believe in your heart is the best for you, what you feel confident in doing and what you feel is the **right thing to do**. Consider other people's feelings and the consequences that your choices will have, but try to make them understand that your decisions were carefully thought of and that you will appreciate their support.

Yes, sometimes you will make mistakes—but if you remain positive and believe in yourself you will learn something valuable from **every single mistake**. 'Whatever happens, happens for the best' is an annoying adage when you hear it, but take it from me—it is bang on target. After a bad choice that seemed like the world's greatest disaster clears up, and you realise it wasn't the apocalypse you believed it to be, the next time you will simply make better decisions!

> *'I have not failed. I've just found 10,000 ways that won't work.'*
>
> —Thomas Alva Edison
> inventor of the phonograph,
> the motion picture camera, and the electric bulb.

Always think carefully and **try to be happy with the choices you have made**, no matter what. Don't drive yourself crazy with 'what ifs' ... *'what if I had done this ... what if I had said yes ... what if I had chosen that course instead?'* Don't waste your time with regret and second-guesses, if you make a mistake, acknowledge it and move on towards your goal.

Simplify your life, so you don't feel overwhelmed by work or relationships. Eliminate unnecessary worries and obligations and find time for yourself. These are all choices you make everyday—so choose to appreciate life! Pursue your goals and dreams and look forward to the future with enthusiasm and optimism. Life can be an adventure if you make the right choices and become a positive thinker. Just do your best and listen to your heart. And remember … stay positive!

> *'The only difference between a good day and a bad day is your attitude.'*
>
> —Dennis S. Brown
>
> President of Destiny Investment. His best-selling motivational tape and attitude T-shirts have been praised by former President Bill Clinton. He tries to ensure that his seminars and speeches increase the performance of his clients.

I quote below an interesting story from an e-book called, *Today is Your Day to Win* by Mike Brescia

'A reporter decided to follow up on an incredible human interest story after hearing of two brothers, one a vicious, dangerous criminal to be locked up for the next ten years for his latest crime, and the other a highly respected university professor.

On his arrest the brother with the criminal record told the police about his university professor brother—his closest living relative. The police tipped an eager reporter that this could be an interesting story. Upon interviewing both men at length, the reporter learned that their father was a brutal man and a hard drinker. His brand of teaching his boys 'right from wrong' included terrible verbal abuse, no matter where they happened to be. When they 'got out of line,' he hit them with belts, his fists, sticks— whatever was handy. They both told almost identical stories of extreme cruelty. Neither one was exempt from the old man's anger and drunken rage.

When the boys were 19 and 20 respectively, their father died of a massive heart attack. Shortly afterwards, the brothers had a falling out and never saw each other again. Brother number one moved out of the state and fell off the face of the earth … living his life between jail terms.

Brother number two graduated from college and followed the designed path to a rewarding life of service to his community, his church and his family. The element that practically knocked the reporter over was both the brothers' identical answer to the same question.

After getting the background on both individuals, the question was, "How did you get to this point in your life?" The two answered the question with the same response: "With a father like mine, how could I be any different?"'

The father was the same but the attitude of the two sons was completely different. The first son blamed his father for everything and used him as an excuse. The other realised that he did not wish to be a replica of his father later in life and used him as motivation–a lesson in life on what was *not* to be done!

This story also highlights how having belief and confidence in yourself can completely change the path your life is on, whereas a lack of self-belief will leave you in a very dissatisfied place. History is replete with stories of heroes who came from very ordinary backgrounds or pious and saintly people who started their lives in very different conditions. It is their attitude and choices that made all the difference.

'Life is a journey ... not a destination.' You have the power to make that journey a beautiful one by appreciating every moment of it, come what may.

So remember, we all have the ability and the freedom to make our choices … make the right ones!

Good choices will boost our self-esteem!

We can decide what is best for us!

So, choose to be aware! choose to be thankful! choose to be happy! And live the best life you can!

The indomitable spirit of Stephen Hawking

Professor Stephen William Hawking was born on 8 January 1942, exactly 300 years after the death of Galileo. From a very early age Hawking showed the qualities of a scientist; he was inquisitive and curious about the world around him, and loved to build models to see how things worked.

In school, Hawking was a keen child, but not the brightest in his competitive A stream class. Though they gave him the nickname 'Einstein', some of his classmates actually did not believe he would succeed in the field of science!

At the age of 20 Hawking went on to do research in cosmology at Cambridge. One day, he lost his balance and fell down a flight of stairs, hitting his head. Worried that he would lose his genius, he took a test to verify that his intellectual abilities were intact. The test showed that his mental faculties were absolutely fine, but diagnosed something much worse ... a protracted case of Amyotrophic Lateral Sclerosis (ALS), a motor neuron disease, which typically gave him no more than two or three years to live. Hawking gradually lost the use of his arms, legs, and voice, and since 2009 has been almost completely paralysed ... an unbelievably shattering event in anyone's life.

But Hawking did not let that pin him down and continued to research and travel, finding answers to the burning questions of the science that he loved so much. However, during a visit to the research centre CERN (European Organisation for Nuclear Research, translated in English) in Geneva, Switzerland in 1985, Hawking contracted pneumonia. This was a terrible development, because, in Hawking's condition, pneumonia was life-threatening as it further restricted his already limited respiratory capacity. Hawking had an emergency tracheotomy, and as a result lost whatever remained of his ability to speak. Since then, he has used an electronic voice synthesiser to communicate, a cumbersome device which makes talking a tedious drawn-out process.

But, despite all these problems, Hawking describes himself as lucky! He claims the disease's slow progression has allowed him time to make influential discoveries, and is thankful that it has not hindered him from having, in his own words, 'a very attractive family.' Despite facing immense physical challenges, Hawking continues to lecture around the world, has made ground-breaking research, written widely acclaimed books on the cosmos, and continues to be remembered for his intelligence and passion for science, not for his disease. Hawking chose the kind of life he wished to lead, took the initiative and led it, and as a consequence, is today respected and revered not only for his formidable genius, but for his indomitable spirit as well.

> *'Nothing splendid has even been achieved except by those who dared believe that something inside of them was superior to circumstances.'*
>
> —Bruce Barton
> American author,
> advertising executive and politician.

Magic Mantra Four

I AM WORTHY OF LOVE

Magic Mantra Four

I am worthy of love

Creating a healthy self-image

> *You, yourself, as much as anybody else in the entire universe deserves your love and affection.*
>
> —Buddha

Do you have a healthy self-esteem?

Healthy self-esteem means generally liking yourself just the way you are. It does NOT mean feeling perfect, it just means being comfortable in your own skin and being confident about the person you are.

Bouts of self-doubt are perfectly normal even if you have healthy self-esteem, but these bouts should not be so extreme that you keep swinging from feeling great to feeling absolutely worthless.

Healthy self-esteem does not imply *over*-confidence. A person with healthy self-esteem will be confident without being overbearing. Criticism from a third person will not affect him to such a great extent. He won't mind being questioned and is not excessively defensive. He is self-reliant, active and achievement-orientated, without being obsessive because he knows he is not defined solely by his achievements.

It is interesting to note that over-achievers often do *not* have high self-esteem. They are constantly trying to push harder just to be able to overcome their feeling of low self-esteem! People with healthy self-esteem are usually happy with their own selves and capable of withstanding defeats, setbacks and obstacles. People with healthy self-esteem find it easy to laugh at themselves!

Happiness and self-esteem go hand in hand

You could be unhappy due to various external factors like relationships, career, finances, how you look, a recent setback, boredom, being criticised, or any of the myriad challenges that life throws at you.

However, if you have healthy self-esteem, your emotional balance and confidence will hold you in good stead and several of these situations will pass by without causing any deep misery!

Self-esteem means appreciating yourself and knowing that the path ahead is not easy, but being confident that you will be able to cope. Self-esteem is the confidence to be who you are, all the time. And this confidence must arise out of an *honest, realistic* evaluation of your achievements.

Do you have low self-esteem? Are you constantly finding fault not only with yourself but also with the world around you? Do you often think you will fail at something even before you try it? Do you feel life is moving too fast for you, while others seem to cope with it easily? Are you often jealous?

First of all, you must realise that life is tough on *everyone*. There are just people who have learnt to handle it better, and there is no reason why you should not be one of them!

But to do so, you first need to understand the **reason** behind your low self-esteem so you can get over it.

Low self-esteem can stem from a number of causes. If you received continuous criticism as a child, you may now constantly doubt whether you can achieve anything. You may be afraid to venture forth into anything new and prefer to stay in safe and familiar territory!

Our parents, teachers and elders are often perfectionists in their own ways and may have tried to foist their own ideas of life upon us. This could result in a pattern of altered behaviour where you behave timidly and cannot assert yourself, especially when you are overly dependent on others to look after you. You now find ways of escaping unpleasant realities and put very little effort into any activity because you doubt you can be successful. The end result is that you put **yourself** down constantly, and hold **yourself** back!

A major failure could also be a disheartening setback that has eroded your confidence. The important thing to remember here is that everyone messes up, and that as long as you learn from your mistakes, you'll have no regrets. After all, it's not whether you get knocked down, but whether you get up again—that counts!

> *'Success is not final, failure is not fatal: it is the courage to continue that counts.'*
>
> —Sir Winston Leonard-Spencer Churchill
> former British Prime Minister during World War II
> (1940-45) and during 1951-55, an excellent orator.

Low self-esteem can also be brought on when we make the grave mistake of comparing how we feel with how others behave. Inevitably, most others will behave more happily than we feel. So we conclude that no one else is as miserable as we are, and start feeling alone and persecuted!

This feeling of isolation triggers a vicious circle and our self-esteem drops further. Dwelling on the negative is an addiction. Negativity spreads and festers and gets worse. *Nothing is good … nothing is as it should be … everything could be better … life is so unfair to me … I hate my life …* Sounds familiar? It's pretty hard to force yourself to think positively when you are accustomed to feeling so negative!

The solution is to change your attitude

One way to do this is to simply list all the good things you can find in any situation. This may be hard at first, and perhaps someone can help you initially.

Another way is to remember a happy time or incident in your life, when you felt really good about yourself. Let this feeling linger in your mind for a while, and then try to face your 'rotten situation' again.

You will realise that your 'bad feeling' soon disperses and you won't have to resort to blaming everyone and everything around you just to feel better! Congratulations! This means you've found a more positive way of viewing yourself and your situation! Avoid global, all-or-nothing statements like 'everything is wrong with me!'

You're saying you dislike *everything* about yourself, that there is *nothing* to like about you, while in fact, you're unhappy with just one or two traits in your entire personality! There are traits in each one of us that we are not proud of. Rather than focusing on these negative aspects of your personality it is more important to realise that you are blessed with good traits too.

You need to change how **you view yourself**. You are the sum total of all your attributes. When people meet you for the first time they don't look at you piecemeal; they see your overall personality and respond to the vibes that you give out. If you give out loving, positive vibes people will respond to you with the same kind of warmth.

However, if you approach people with a scared look or a defiant expression, then they will respond in the same manner! When you walk into a room, make eye contact with people and smile, and people will reach out to you. If you enter with your head down and skulk around the corners then you will find that people will also avoid talking to you. Body language cannot always be feigned and very often it is a true representative of what is going on in your mind! People subconsciously pick up and respond to our body language. So be happy, be confident, be natural and *smile*!

If you really want to reach out to people and make friends, there are a few qualities that you must develop first. Being a good listener and appreciating people would be somewhere at the top of that list! If you respond sympathetically to people they will react warmly to you; and being liked by people will definitely make you feel much better about yourself!

List what you like about yourself

Have you tried making a list of all your likeable qualities? Think of your strengths—all the things you find easy that others struggle to do. Then think about the things you enjoy doing—chances are you're good at them too! Avoid discounting your strengths by saying, 'that's nothing' or 'anyone can do that.' What about things you have done for others?

Ask your friends or family what they think you are better at than others, or about the times you have helped them in any way.

The following story illustrates a simple point very effectively—that it is important to do a reality check once in a while and see exactly what we are contributing and achieving! So while evaluating yourself, look for feedback from your immediate environment!

There once lived an old lady in a remote village, somewhat cut off from civilisation. Every morning, this lady noted proudly that the only rooster for miles around would stand on the fence of her compound wall and crow loudly! This made her smug, and she would loudly claim to everyone around her that her rooster's crow made the sun rise every morning! She nagged all the villagers to thank her and her rooster for the sunshine the villagers enjoyed every day! The villagers ignored the mad old lady and laughed at her, and

this infuriated her! It was only when her rooster died that she realised the sun still rose and set like it did earlier, regardless of the rooster's crowing! She had spent her life with an inflated idea of her achievements and wasted so many precious moments in bitter thought, when she believed her neighbours did not appreciate her! If only she had asked people what they thought she was good at, she may have learned that even if the sun didn't rise because of her, her neighbours thought she was a brilliant cook, or an exceptional storyteller, or even a nurturing healer!

So, it's important to keep a realistic self-image and to ask people you love and trust what they think you are good at—you never know what gems you'll find in yourself!

To maintain healthy self-esteem you also have to learn to forgive yourself for your mistakes, and to stop judging yourself harshly. Don't allow people to criticise you constantly. Set achievable targets and get regular feedback from people you trust. Give yourself positive pep talks and set reasonable standards for your goals.

If you feel that your self-esteem is low because you are dissatisfied with your looks, and you spend all your time moaning and groaning about it—then you will actually *drive people away*, many of whom may not even have noticed your looks in the first place! If, instead, you focus on being nice to people, they will respond to your warmth and make you forget your dissatisfaction about your looks! Plus, seriously, if you eat healthy food, get good exercise and smile a lot, most of your problems with looks can easily be resolved. Also, please keep in mind that basing your confidence on looks is a losing strategy for happiness. Good looks may attract people initially but they don't last. Ultimately, how you lead your life and whether you choose to be happy or not depends on what is inside you.

A simple thing that you could do to stay positive is to try to avoid dwelling on what makes you unhappy, and keep busy instead! Find out what it is that you really enjoy doing and go out and do it to the best of your ability. Achievement is one of the surest ways of building better self-esteem. Feeling sorry for yourself and brooding over perceived failures is one of the surest ways of staying down. The feeling and glow that you will get out of achieving something will give your self-esteem a tremendous boost!

Another terrific mood elevator is physical exercise, which actually causes your brain to chemically shift towards a happier state! So take up a sport, join a gym, or simply go for a run. Exercise will not only make you feel healthier and look better, which will raise your self-esteem, but it also releases a chemical in the body that is proven to be a mood booster!

Also, do remember that you are not the only person suffering from low self-esteem. Look around you and you'll probably find that other people have bigger problems than yours. Try to cheer up someone else and it will have the double effect of not only spreading some joy, but cheering *you* up as well! Say something nice to someone who's feeling low, talk to someone who's had a bad day, appreciate the hard work of someone who's just experienced failure and watch your own mood bounce back along with your new friend's!

Your guide to accepting and loving yourself

Loving ourselves – being as compassionate, gentle, and loving with ourselves as we would with a best friend – can be pretty hard to do. Very often because we are part of a large family or because of our social or academic environment, we are conditioned to deny our own needs and to take care of others first. On top of that, we're also frequently bombarded with messages telling us not to accept or love ourselves, because we're not good enough.

But it is possible to love ourselves—or at least to increase our self-love in increments, until we can know, deep down to our core, that we're beautiful inside and out.

Here are some of the things that you could do:

Get positive feedback: Sometimes it's interesting to ask people who know you well to discuss you dispassionately. Beware; you might just hear things you don't want to! You may even be surprised to see how well people know you! And I'm sure there will be remarks that will pleasantly surprise you!

Ask friends to send you text or email: If hearing what people like about you is embarrassing, ask your friends to write it down for you, or send you a text or email. This way you can even read it over and over. Go back to it as many times as you can. Whenever you start to hear those critical voices inside your head, go back to those things your friends said or wrote about you and remember that you are loved.

Make a list of positive factors in you: It would also be great to make a list of the things you like about yourself. See if you can look at your life dispassionately and try to be as honest as you can with yourself! If you're having trouble finding things you value about yourself, think about the things you value and love in your friends, then see if those things exist inside you too. You will be surprised to find that very often they do.

Make it a part of your **daily routine** to praise a quality you like about yourself, and don't hold back! It may seem highly improper to be seen praising yourself, but this healing exercise will nourish your self-worth and make your confidence bloom.

Love yourself like a friend

Close your eyes and think of the people you deeply love and trust and whom you know love you—friends or lovers. Think about all the things you love and appreciate about them. Notice how that love feels inside you, how it makes you feel good.

Now turn it the other way around—be *your* friend, feeling that same deep love for *yourself*. See yourself through gentle eyes, with compassion and love, the way your friend does, even if you can only do it for a moment. Now let yourself receive that love, the love you have as a friend to yourself. Feel the warmth move through you. Remember how it feels and come back to that love another time.

Make a note every time someone says something nice about you

Every time someone tells you something about yourself that makes you feel good, write it down or make a mental note and jot it down later. When you get home, put that note in a container of 'good things about me.' Decorate the container whichever way you like. Keep on adding notes and reading them every time you need a little boost—and sometimes even when you don't!

Have compassion for yourself

If you're feeling really judgemental about something you've done or said, try to understand where the judgement is coming from. Not the immediate, surface answer, but an answer deep down inside you.

Are you afraid of something, or are you feeling insecure? Do you think you did something 'wrong,' or are you hearing the judgement of a voice from your past? Try to connect to that little child inside you who's feeling that way and listen to the voice. Hug and reassure that child saying that no wrong was committed and that you love her/him.

You could also think of a friend acting the way you did. Imagine how you'd feel towards them—how you'd still love them and readily forgive them, if there was anything to forgive. You probably wouldn't even find it bothersome! Try to feel that same love and compassion for *yourself*!

Recognise that the love has to come from you

If you're a survivor of child abuse or come from a dysfunctional family, you may still be waiting for a parent to give you the love and acceptance you never got as a child. But the kind of love you need (or needed as a child) probably isn't going to come from a parent who abused you or who looked the other way while you were being abused. But it can come from *you*.

It can be hard to give it to yourself at first; after all, if you didn't receive love as a child, or if some of that love was torn away from you by violence, self-hate may have built up inside you. But you have the courage and strength to love yourself, if you've survived this long. And you do deserve it! So try to connect to that little child inside, that child who deserves all of your love and acceptance. And then *give him or her* all the love and acceptance you are capable of.

Comfort and nurture yourself

Allow yourself to do comforting and nurturing things for yourself. Allow yourself to feel really good when you do those things and tell yourself that you deserve to feel that way! Gradually you'll find that the more nurturing and comforting times you have, the more you'll seek them out—and finally they will help build a good feeling inside you.

Ask yourself what you need to do

Some of these ideas will work really well for you, while others may not quite fit. So try taking a quiet moment to ask yourself, 'What can I do to feel more compassion and love towards myself?' Don't force an answer; just let the answer bubble up from inside you. If you find it hard to hear the answer that way, try writing out your question and then your answer. See what you come up with. Only you know best what works for you. *Trust me; you have great wisdom inside you.*

Appreciation goes a long way!

A teacher in New York decided to honour each of her senior high school students by telling them the difference each of them made.

Using a process developed by Helice Bridges of Del Mar, California, she called each student to the front of the class, one at a time.

First she told them how the student made a difference to her and the class. Then she presented each of them with a blue ribbon imprinted with the golden words, 'Who I Am Makes a Difference.'

Later on, this teacher decided to do a class project to see what kind of impact 'recognition' would have on a community.

She gave each of the students three more ribbons and instructed them to go out and spread this acknowledgement ceremony further. They were to follow up on the results, see who honoured whom and report back to the class in about a week.

One of the boys in the class went to a junior executive in a nearby company and honoured him for helping him with his career planning. He gave him a blue ribbon and put it on his shirt.

Then he gave him two extra ribbons, and said, 'We're doing a class project on recognition, and we'd like you to go out, find somebody to honour and give a blue ribbon, then hand over the extra blue ribbon as well so that this person can acknowledge a third person to keep this acknowledgement ceremony rolling. Then please report back to me and tell me what happened.'

Later that day the junior executive went in to see his boss, who was quite notably a grouchy fellow. He sat his boss down and told him that he deeply admired him for being a creative genius. The boss seemed very surprised. The junior executive asked him if he would accept the gift of the blue ribbon and would he give him permission to put it on him. His surprised boss said, 'Well, sure.'

The junior executive took the blue ribbon and placed it right on his boss's jacket above his heart. As he gave him the last extra ribbon, he said, 'Would you do me a favour? Would you take this extra ribbon and pass it on by honouring somebody else? The young boy who first gave me the ribbons is doing a project in school and we want to keep this recognition ceremony going and find out how it affects people.'

That night the boss came home to his 14-year-old son and sat him down. He said, 'The most incredible thing happened to me today. I was in my office and one of the junior executives came in and told me he admired me and gave me a blue ribbon for being a creative genius. Imagine. He thinks I'm a creative genius!

'Then he put this blue ribbon that says, "Who I Am Makes a Difference" on my jacket above my heart. He gave me an extra ribbon and asked me to find somebody else to honour. As I was driving home tonight, I started thinking about whom I would honour with this ribbon and I thought about you. I want to honour you.

'My days are really hectic and when I come home I don't pay too much attention to you. Sometimes I scream at you for not getting good grades in school and for your bedroom being a mess, but somehow tonight I just wanted to sit here and, well, just let you know that you do make a difference in my life. Besides your mother, you are the most important person in my life. You're a great kid and I love you!' The startled boy started to sob and sob, and he couldn't stop crying. His whole body shook.

He looked up at his father and said through his tears, 'I was planning to commit suicide tomorrow, Dad, because I didn't think you loved me. Now I don't need to.'

(Helice Bridges was known as 'The First Lady of Acknowledgement' and the 'Mother Teresa of Self-Esteem').

Magic Mantra Five

I WILL SET MY GOALS AND DESIGN MY FUTURE

Magic Mantra Five

I will set my goals and design my future

Charting a map to your dream

> *Good fortune is what happens when opportunity meets with planning!*
>
> —Thomas Alva Edison

You have just reached a new city and you don't know a soul. You come out of the railway station, hail a taxi and board it. The taxi driver is quick to realise that you are not in familiar surroundings and that it would be the easiest thing in the world to make a fast buck out of you! So, what does he do? He simply turns his FM radio on and drives you round and round the city in circles! Now while this is happening you are so immersed in absorbing all the details of the new city outside, or calling your family and friends to tell them where you are, that by the time you realise what's going on, the taxi driver has taken you far away from your destination!

This situation is a bit like setting forth on a journey without your map. You put the car in gear and off you go. Down the road you realise that you need to check the map because you've reached an intersection you're not familiar with. So you look into the glove compartment, then under your seat, but you can't find it; and then it hits you that you've left it behind! So, now you panic! You know where you're going—the only thing that you

don't know is how to actually get there! You take a right and then you turn left, and then turn right again, change the radio station and keep on going. Unfortunately, you never reach your destination.

You may know what your final destination is but unless you have some idea of the address, the locality, or directions to get there, you could keep going round and round in circles. The journey may take you a very long time because the instructions that you get along the way may not be accurate, or the people you ask for directions may be confident, yet totally wrong! Even today's sophisticated GPRS systems won't work unless you feed in the correct address!

If you don't know where you're going, you will wind up travelling in circles! The solution is to clearly articulate and communicate your destination, and then to break it down into achievable, recognisable milestones or landmarks. This way, you're sure to get to your destination faster and in a much, much happier state of mind!

> *'Our plans miscarry because they have no aim. When a man does not know what harbour he is making for, no wind is the right wind.'*
>
> —Seneca
> Roman Stoic philosopher,
> statesman and dramatist.

Too many of us treat goal-setting the same way. We daydream about where we want to be, but we don't plan on how to get there. What is the difference between a dream and a goal? It is simply the clarity of the written word—a map! Goal setting means putting down clear directions to a desired destination on a piece of paper. It's quite simply your map to success!

Setting goals will help you decide what you want to achieve in your life and separate what is important from what is irrelevant. Setting goals will motivate you and build your self-confidence as you progress towards fulfilling your dreams.

'A goal properly set is halfway reached.'

—Abraham Lincoln

Setting goals effectively

The following broad guidelines will help you to set effective goals:

Set your own goals: These are your goals for your life. Do not ask someone else to set your goals for you; they need to stem from your interests, desires, and ambitions. You will be truly motivated to work only towards a goal that *you* want to achieve.

'The biggest mistake people make in life is not trying to make a living doing what they most enjoy.'

—Malcolm Stevenson Forbes
publisher of *Forbes* magazine founded by his father
B.C. Forbes—a Scottish immigrant to America.
Malcolm was known for his lavish spending on
parties, travel, and his collection of homes, yachts,
aircraft, and art.

It's possible that you have no clue about what you want to do. In that case, look around you and see what others are doing, and if something appears interesting to you, maybe that's what your goal should be!

State each goal as a positive statement: Express your goals positively–'Score more than 80 per cent' is much better than 'Don't make these stupid mistakes'. Work for what you want, not for what you want to leave behind. Part of the reason behind why we write down and examine our goals is to create a set of instructions for our subconscious mind to carry out. Your subconscious mind is a very efficient tool, it cannot tell right from wrong and it does not judge. Its only function is to carry out its instructions. So, the more detailed instructions you give it, the more positive results you will get. It's really that simple.

Be precise: Set a precise goal, putting in dates and times for expected milestones of achievement so that you can measure your progress. If you do this, you will know exactly when you have achieved your goal and can be completely satisfied with your hard work and progress.

Provide enough detail about what exactly you should be doing to achieve your goal. A goal of 'study biology' is vague. Should you be reading your text? If so, what pages? Or should you be looking over your lecture notes? A much better goal would be: 'Read pages 12-35 in the biology textbook, write questions in the margin, and practise answering those questions after reading.'

It may sound silly, but you should write even your lifetime goals in *complete detail*. Instead of simply writing – 'A new home' – fill in details that you visualise or dream of, such as 'A 4,000 sq ft contemporary with four bedrooms and three bathrooms and a view of the mountain on 20 acres of land.' Once again we are giving the subconscious mind a detailed set of instructions to work on. The more information you give it, the clearer the vision becomes. And the more precise the vision, the more efficiently the subconscious mind works! Can you close your eyes and visualise the home I described above? Walk around this house. Stand on the porch of the master bedroom and see the fog lifting off the mountain. Look down at the garden full of tomatoes, green beans and cucumbers. And, off to the right, is the other garden full of chrysanthemums, carnations and roses. Can you see it? Can you smell the cool, fresh air and the fruity scents? So can your subconscious mind; it will work day and night to give you all you desire.

Set priorities: When you have several goals, give each a priority. This helps you avoid feeling overwhelmed by too many goals and helps to direct your attention to the most important ones. Too many goals without a priority will cause you to go berserk and ultimately burnout. Appreciate that there's a time to work hard, and there's a time to sit back and relax. Remember to give yourself time to unwind and just enjoy life; that's an important aspect of living as well!

Write goals down: Writing down your goals crystallises them and gives them energy. Your written goals create the roadmap to your success. Sometimes, just the act of writing them down can set the process in motion!

Keep operational goals small: Keep low-level goals small and achievable. If a goal is too large, then it can seem like you are not making enough progress towards it. Keeping goals small and incremental gives you more opportunities to reward your hard work. Derive today's smaller goals from life's larger ones.

Set performance goals, not outcome goals: This is very, very important. Take care to set goals over which you have as much control as possible. There is nothing more dispiriting than failing to achieve a goal for reasons beyond your control. These could be bad business environments, poor judgement, unpredictable weather, injury, or just plain bad luck. If you base your goals on *personal* performance, then you can keep control over the achievements you have made and draw satisfaction from them, irrespective of the actual outcome.

Set Measurable Goals: Your goal should be such that, when you are through, you have some tangible evidence of completion. It feels good to see something in front of you that indicates a job well done. For example, if your goal is simply to 'Read Chapter 3', the end result cannot be reliably assessed. Did you fully understand the words when you looked at the pages? A much better goal would be: 'Read Chapter 3 and then write a summary from memory'. The summary would indicate that you in fact did read the chapter and would allow you to evaluate your degree of understanding. Producing tangible evidence requires **active** studying on your part, which obviously results in superior learning and retention.

Set realistic goals: It is important to set goals that you *can* achieve. All sorts of people – including your parents, society, and the media – can set unrealistic goals for you. Alternatively, you may be naïve and set very high goals for yourself. You might not appreciate either the obstacles on the way, or understand quite how many skills you must master to achieve a particular level of performance. Then, when you realise your goal is unrealistic you will automatically lose the motivation to put in serious effort towards achieving it.

This is not to say that you should refrain from setting high goals, quite the opposite. The experience of goal setting is terrific when the goal is set high, you have a fairly clear understanding of what steps are required to be taken to get there, and are capable of following through with those steps.

However, also understand that your belief that a goal is unrealistic may be incorrect! If this is the case, you can change your mindset with positive thinking and effective visualisation.

Don't plan to do things if you are unlikely to follow through! It is better to plan only a few things and be successful rather than overburden yourself and feel like a failure. Success breeds success! Start small with what you can do. Experience the joys of meeting your goal and only then gradually increase the amount of work that you ask of yourself. Setting goals in which every minute of the day is accounted for is unrealistic; unplanned events will crop up and wreak havoc with your schedule. Give yourself some flexibility.

Also, when you put all your goals down on paper, ascertain whether any of your goals are in conflict with each other. Goals and dreams are different. You may dream of buying a mansion with a huge garden, but if the cost is five times beyond what you will be able to afford according to your career path, then your career goals and home-owning goals are not feasible together. Setting conflicting goals is called non-integrated thinking and will sabotage the hard work you put into your plans; so strive to eliminate contradictory ideas from your goal setting.

By all means, make sure your goal is high: Aim for the stars; if you miss you'll still land on the moon! It is just as important not to set goals unrealistically high as to set them too low. People tend to do this when they are afraid of failure or if they're simply lazy! You should set goals so that they are slightly out of your immediate grasp, but not so far that there is no hope of achieving them. That's the perfect balance that will keep you motivated, challenged and inspired.

> *'Our goals can only be reached through the vehicle of a plan–in which we must fervently believe, and upon which we must vigorously act. There is no other route to success.'*
>
> —Vincent van Gogh
>
> Dutch post-impressionist artist.

Goal setting techniques are used extensively by top-level athletes, successful business-people, and achievers in all fields. Goal setting gives you both long-term vision as well as short-term motivation. Your goals are set on a number of different levels. You first decide what you want to do with your life and what large-scale goals you want to achieve. Second, you break these down into the smaller and smaller targets that you must hit so that you reach your lifetime goals. Finally, once you have your plan, you start working towards achieving it. So, let's begin.

Lifetime goals

The first step in setting personal goals is to consider what you want to achieve in your lifetime, as setting lifetime goals gives you the overall perspective that shapes all your other decisions.

To give a broad, balanced coverage of all the important areas in your life, try to set goals in some or all of the following categories:

Career: Where do you see yourself five years from today, where do you see yourself 10 years from today, or maybe 20 years from today? What level do you want to reach in your career?

Education: Would you like to pursue a college education? Do you see yourself as a professional—a doctor or a computer specialist? Do you see yourself as an artist, a teacher, a business executive, or a chef? Is there any field of knowledge you would like to specialise in? What information and skills would you need to achieve your other goals?

Family: Do you see yourself with a large family? What kind of spouse are you looking for? Do you see small children playing in the garden?

Financial: How much do you want to earn and at what stage? Do you see the kind of house you will own or the kind of cars parked in your driveway? Do you see the kind of vacations you could go on?

Physical: Are there athletic goals you want to achieve? Do you see yourself living in perfectly good health to a ripe old age? Do you see yourself maintaining your fitness? What steps are you going to take to achieve this?

Once you've decided your goals in categories broadly like the ones above, you should assign priorities to them, ranging from 'most immediate' to 'not so immediate'. Then review the goals and re-prioritise until you are satisfied that they reflect the shape of the life you want to lead. Once you've set your lifetime goals, set a 25-year plan of smaller goals that you should complete if you are to reach your lifetime plan. Then set a five-year plan, a one-year plan, a six-month plan, and a month plan—progressively smaller goals that you should reach to achieve your lifetime goals. Each of these should be derived from the previous, larger goals. Finally, you will be able to set a **daily to-do list** of things that will slowly take you towards your lifetime goals! At an early stage these goals may be simply to gather information about your plans. That's fine; this will help you to improve the quality and realism of your goal setting pattern.

Finally, review your plans and make sure that they reflect the way you want to live your life.

Setting your own goals—a guide

Here are some questions you could answer to help you narrow down your goals:

- What are my short-term goals and long-term desired outcomes?
- What has been happening to my personal relationships?
- Am I open enough with other people? Do I talk to them about my problems and my feelings? Do I share my anxieties, my fears, and my frustrations?
- Do I do enough physical exercise? What can I do about this?
- Am I too tense? Should I learn some relaxation techniques?
- Do I eat too much or too little? Should I change my eating habits?
- Do I drink too much or too little? Should I change my drinking habits?
- Do I smoke? Is it time to give up?

- How might I incorporate some time management techniques into my life?
- Do I automatically take on extra work when asked? What would happen if I learned to say 'No'?

Now consider the questions carefully, giving no less than ten minutes of thought to each question. Then write your answers down next to each question. Then go through your answers, one by one, again giving no less than ten minutes of thought to each answer.

Have you been totally honest with yourself?

If you have, good. You can move on to the next stage of taking charge of your life!

So your goals are written down. What's the next step?
Negative comments from friends, family, and neighbours can drag you down very quickly. It's very important that your self-talk (the thoughts in your head) remain positive, and that no one talks you out of following your dreams. At this point, you need to believe in yourself and in the power of your dreams.

> *'Don't ask what the world needs. Ask what makes you come alive, and go do it. Because what the world needs is people who have come alive.'*
>
> —Howard Thurman
> American theologian,
> scholar and civil rights mentor.

Reviewing your goals daily is crucial to your success and must become part of your routine. Each morning when you wake up, read your list of goals. Visualise the completed goal, see your new home, hear the applause for your work, feel the happiness of being with your family and loved ones, feel the rush of an exciting new assignment. Then each night, right before you go to bed, repeat the process. This routine will trigger both your subconscious and conscious mind to work towards your goal. This will also begin to replace any negative self-talk you may have with positive affirmations.

> *'Set out each day believing in your dreams. Know without a doubt that you were made for amazing things.*
>
> —Josh Hinds
>
> inspirational speaker, author and entrepreneur.

Nothing in life can be achieved without hard work. To make your dreams a reality, you will now need to work at making them come true! Writing down crystal clear goals was the first step; now it's time to step up and prove your determination and passion to succeed. Here is a story:

A stable owner once bought the fastest horse in the whole world. He made a grand placard declaring that this was the fastest horse ever, and put it up at the horse's stable for the world to see. He never let his precious horse out for a run; for fear that it would get injured! After a few months, the horse was brought forth for an important race. The stable owner was sure it would win; it was the fastest horse in the world after all! However, the 'fastest horse' had now spent many months like a showpiece in his master's stable and was slow and out of practice ... and it was left far behind on the race track.

This story teaches us that *only* positive thinking will not get you far, you also need to work hard to achieve your dreams. With a combination of goal setting, dedication, and optimism, you can win in life!

Staying on course

Once you have decided on your first set of plans, keep the process going by reviewing your goals frequently. Remember, the more focused you are on your goals, the more likely you are to accomplish them.

Sometimes you may realise you have to revise a goal as circumstances and your other goals change. If this happens, do not consider it a failure; consider it a victory that you had the insight to realise something needed to be changed! Life keeps changing and you learn more every day. It is also a healthy sign if your goals change as you mature! Update your to-do list daily to incorporate new goals and ideas you may nurture.

To be able to really stay on course, every time you make a decision you should ask yourself this question, 'Does it take me closer to, or further away from my goal?' If the answer is 'closer to,' then you've made the right decision. If your answer is 'further from' … well, you know what to do!

Achieving goals

Whenever you achieve a goal, however small, take the time to enjoy the satisfaction of success. Absorb the implications of your achievement, and observe the progress you have made towards your other goals. If the goal achieved was a significant one, reward your hard work appropriately!

> *Remember: 'Never give up on your dream … perseverance is all important. If you don't have the desire and the belief*

in yourself to keep trying after you've been told you should quit, you'll never make it.'

—Tawni O' Dell

the *New York Times* bestselling author of *Fragile Beasts, Sister Mine, Coal Run,* and *Back Roads,* which was an Oprah's Book Club pick.

Here's the story of a revolutionary man who knew what he wanted and worked hard towards his dream, letting nothing stop him … not even 27 years in prison!

Building the world of your dreams—the story of Nelson Mandela

In 1948, the apartheid policy of racial segregation was at fever pitch in South Africa. The Afrikaans' dominated National Party had been elected to power, which staunchly supported apartheid, and blacks were ruthlessly discriminated against. It was during these turbulent times that the 30-year-old Nelson Mandela began actively participating in politics.

Nelson was greatly influenced by the teachings of Mahatma Gandhi and was a firm believer in non-violent movements. In 1961, however, when it became clear that peaceful demonstrations were not making any considerable impact towards ending apartheid, Mandela changed his tactics. He began to coordinate sabotage campaigns against military and government targets, making plans for his last resort—guerrilla warfare.

In 1962, he launched a guerrilla attack that caused the government to sit up and take notice. Mandela then lived on the run for 17 months, till he was finally found and arrested. He was then put on trial for sabotage and treason.

During his trial, Mandela's statement from the dock closed with these powerful words—'During my lifetime I have dedicated myself to the struggle of the African people. I have fought against white domination, and I have fought against black domination. I have cherished the ideal of a democratic and free society in which all persons live together in harmony and with equal opportunities. It is an ideal which I hope to live for and to achieve. But if need be, it is an ideal for which I am prepared to die.'

He was found guilty. However, Mandela luckily escaped the gallows and was sentenced to life imprisonment on 12 July 1964.

Mandela was imprisoned in Robben Island for the first 18 years of his sentence. Prison conditions on Robben Island were very harsh. The prisoners performed hard labour in a lime quarry and were segregated according to race, with black prisoners receiving the fewest rations! Political prisoners were kept separate from ordinary prisoners and received even fewer privileges! Mandela later described how he was allowed one visitor and one letter every six months. Letters, when they came, were often delayed and made unreadable by prison censors.

Most people would have lost hope in such maddening conditions, but Nelson was determined to use even his time in prison productively! He undertook a correspondence course with the University of London and earned his Bachelor of Law degree! 'We must use time wisely and forever realise that the time is always ripe to do right,' he said.

While in jail, Mandela's reputation grew till he became the most significant black leader in South Africa. So much so that the authorities began to fear his influence on the new generation of black activists on Robben Island, and took a decision to transfer him to another prison.

In 1985, Mandela was offered a chance to get out of prison by President Botha. There was only one condition, he must agree to 'unconditionally reject violence as a political weapon.' Nelson refused this offer and issued a statement through his daughter saying, 'What freedom am I being offered while the organisation of the people remains banned? Only free men can negotiate. A prisoner cannot enter into contracts.'

Throughout Mandela's imprisonment, local and international pressure mounted on the South African government to release him, under the resounding slogan 'Free Nelson Mandela!' In 1989, President Botha suffered a stroke and was replaced by Frederik Willem de Klerk. De Klerk announced Mandela's release in February 1990.

On the momentous day of his release, Mandela emerged after 27 long years in prison and made a speech to the nation. He declared his commitment to peace and reconciliation with the country's white minority, but he also made it clear that the ANC's armed struggle would not cease till the reason for their struggle was addressed. He also declared that his main focus was still to bring peace to the black majority and give them the right to vote in both national and local elections. Even 27 years in prison had not dimmed his passion for justice or his conviction in his beliefs!

And finally, on 27 April 1994, Nelson's vision became reality. On that day, South Africa's first multi-racial elections were held, in which full enfranchisement was granted. Nelson Mandela had freed his people and given them their rights.

During this landmark election of 1994, the African National Congress was elected to power. Mandela, as leader of the ANC, became the country's first 'black' President on 10 May 1994.

Over the last 40 years, Mandela has won over 250 awards for his exemplary work, including the 1993 Nobel Peace Prize. And even today, Nelson Mandela continues to be a worldwide symbol of integrity and compassion, and a beacon of hope for justice and equality.

Nelson Mandela went through an unbelievably difficult struggle to fulfill his dream. There must have been so many times when it would have seemed easier to give up. But he strove with a single-minded dedication towards his vision and made it come true.

Remember the words of Nelson Mandela whenever you feel like giving up on your dreams: *'I learned that courage was not the absence of fear, but the triumph over it. The brave man is not he who does not feel afraid, but he who conquers that fear.'*

Magic Mantra Six

I DREAM BIG AND BELIEVE IN THE POWER OF MY DREAMS!

Magic Mantra Six

I dream big and believe in the power of my dreams!

Creative visualisation

> *The best way to predict the future is to create it.*
>
> —Peter Ferdinand Drucker
>
> Austrian-born American management consultant, educator, and author. His writings contributed to the philosophical and practical foundations of the modern business corporation.

Do you know that you can *literally* make your dreams come true by using the power of your mind? That stunning process, in a nut-shell, is what Creative Visualisation is all about.

What exactly is Creative Visualisation?

Creative Visualisation is looking at yourself as the person you *want to be*. It is placing yourself in situations now, which you dream of being in the future. This is really simple, and I'll explain this with the help of a real-life example. Once a friend came to me saying she passionately wanted to be a writer but she had a problem in actually getting started. I advised her to start attending writers' conferences, hang out and discuss literature with other writers and follow a professional writer's work-routine by writing something *every day*. I basically advised her to start behaving like she was *already* a writer! So she made friends with a group of authors and simply started living a writer's life! As she spent time with these writers and kept them company socially, she absorbed *everything* about the lifestyle, engagements and commitments of a real life writer! She constantly listened to these writers' achievements, how they handled their work, how they sold manuscripts and all the tricks of the trade ... and her mind automatically made her the writer she always wanted to be! I am happy to tell you that she is now a successfully published author! By simply placing herself as a successful writer in her own mind, she managed to achieve her ambition!

So if you want to be successful, make friends and mix with the people you consider icons in the field you want to succeed in, and *learn everything*. Stay close to your dream so that you see it every day; so that you *live it* every day. This will set your mind in motion and it will work fervently to achieve your dream.

Creative Visualisation is *also* using your powerful imagination to see clear images in your mind ... and to make these images come true!

Once a dream is clear in your head and you focus on it, you will feel it and *see it come true in your mind*. These dreams actually become a great creative power that makes things happen! The thought in your mind is the matrix or blueprint; the feelings you invest into your dream provide the energy, the 'electricity' that zaps your dream into reality.

Sounds weird? Not at all!

This is simply the power of Creative Visualisation. Your mind can literally alter your universe! Your thoughts can change your environment and circumstances; attract money, possessions, recognition, interesting work … and even love! Your thoughts can change your habits and improve your health.

Creative Visualisation teaches you to use this immense power of the mind to fulfill your dreams. History is replete with successful people who have used Creative Visualisation techniques and have become legends in their fields.

> *'A man is but the product of his thoughts, and what he thinks, he becomes.'*
>
> —Mahatma Gandhi

Imagine you have a genie at your disposal!

By visualising an event, a situation, or even an object such as a car, a house, or a gadget, you actually attract it to you. You dream intensely about something, achieving it is always on your mind … *and presto–you get it*! This looks and sounds like magic, but it's really not. It's simply the natural power of thought!

> *'If you can dream it, you can do it.'*
>
> —Walt Disney

Have you ever heard of the term 'internal alarm clock'? It's a simple yet wonderful phenomenon that works on the basic principle of visualisation.

A study by Jan Born at the University of Lubeck in Germany found that the body itself *knows* when it is time to wake up and starts releasing 'wake up' chemicals a full

90 minutes before the scheduled wake-up time—without a clock in sight!

I remember my boarding-school days when we didn't have alarm clocks. To wake up then, we devised a simple system that really worked, and that continues to work for me even today! What was that system? Our internal alarm clocks!

So how does one set one's internal alarm clock? It's very simple—when you're in bed, just before you fall asleep, try to convince yourself that you will wake up at a particular time. Create a clear picture in your mind of yourself waking up – fully alert and fresh – at whichever time you choose. In the picture notice yourself rolling over to check your clock and see that you've awoken at the perfect time. See yourself jumping out of bed.

Be sure to imagine a picture of your clock. I've found that this works best as our subconscious minds tend to respond better to pictures and symbols. Make the picture of the time as clear as possible. Tell your subconscious 'This is the time I will wake up!'

As children we used a simpler process called 'the pillow smash!' Before you sleep, use your head to gently *tap your pillow* the same number of times as the hour you want to wake up. You will find that you actually wake up at your chosen time!

So, for example, if you want to get up at 7:00 a.m., tap your pillow seven times just before you go to sleep. Imagine yourself waking up at 7:00. Tell yourself *repeatedly* you will definitely wake up at 7:00 a.m. Please don't be discouraged by how simple these instructions are! When you think about it, you'll realise that it's just common sense to give instructions to your subconscious mind this way!

The last step is: sleep well, and trust yourself enough to give your internal alarm clock a real chance to work!

If you really believe in something, your body will pick up these signals and manifest your thoughts. That's why Creative Visualisation can even be used to feel healthier, or to overcome your fears! For instance, think about what happens when you scare a person by saying there is a huge dog or a rat in the room. Their bodies react to the stimulus, their hearts start beating faster and adrenaline is pumped into their blood streams. But there may not actually be a dog or a rat in the room! The body doesn't need visual confirmation to react; just thinking about the object of fear will bring on perspiration and a thumping heart! What if you use this power of the mind over the body to make yourself healthier, braver and happier instead? Use this wonderful relationship between your mind and body to your advantage!

Understanding Creative Visualisation and the power of thought

How and why does Creative Visualisation work?

It works on the simple premise that **thought** is a force that has an effect on the material world. Thought actually travels, filtering through the molecules and atoms floating around our world, and the more intense the thought, the more it gets through to other particles. If we keep thinking the same thought, people in our environment sense it and act on it, furthering the materialisation of our desires!

For example, when I find myself about to confront an unpleasant situation, I visualise myself handling the matter easily and comfortably. I see the people involved being cooperative and friendly. And do you know what happens? The people do turn out to be pleasant and eager to help without even being asked! People are responsive to our thoughts, feelings and behavior and react accordingly! If you are naturally a positive person, then the way you approach and handle situations automatically attracts positive results. On the other hand, if you are fearful and negative, then you expect negative results, and behave and talk accordingly. That's when you reap trouble.

So why does Creative Visualisation work?

Thought is energy. When we concentrate on our thoughts, we make them stronger by infusing them with emotion and desire. These thoughts affect the energy fields around us, causing them to move and act. You must have heard the phrase 'I got a good vibe from him.' What is this vibe? It's the energy of our thoughts reaching out to others! The vibes our thoughts give out, affect the energy balance of people, objects, and situations around us, moulding our environment according to our vibes!

> *'You create your own universe as you go along.'*
>
> —Sir Winston Leonard Spencer-Churchill
>
> Prime Minister of the United Kingdom (1940-1945; 1951-1955). Widely regarded as one of the greatest

wartime leaders of the 20th century.
Only British Prime Minister to have received the
Nobel Prize in Literature.

There is another explanation as to why Creative Visualisation works. It may come as a surprise, but the theory of 'Maya'or 'Illusion' – which comes from eastern philosophies – provides a reason for Creative Visualisation and its impact on reality.

According to Indian philosophy and the *Advaita-Vedanta,* the world is just an illusion and is not real. Our thoughts actually 'create' our world. We constantly think and rethink our habitual thoughts, thus creating and recreating the same kind of events or circumstances. This seemingly unchanging world only reinforces our thoughts, which again helps preserve the same 'world' we believe we live in. By changing our thoughts, we actually create our different 'reality'!

When we change our thoughts, the illusion we live in changes, and a new illusion becomes our reality … directed by our thoughts! It is like dreaming a very realistic dream and then switching to a different dream. We are not waking up; we are just changing the dream. This explanation may have to be read, reread and pondered upon in order to understand its full meaning.

Albert Einstein, a firm believer in creative visualisation, said, 'Your imagination is your preview of life's coming attractions.'

Rest assured that you can still employ the power of Creative Visualisation, even if you do not accept what you have just read, or if it seems too complicated or far-fetched. Yet, understanding and accepting the above, at least in theory, will help you achieve results faster.

So, what we dream about is what we get, right?

Right! So why not change your dreams to something more satisfying? For example, you may be living in a small apartment and need a larger one. Instead of cursing your fate, moaning over the fact that you haven't enough money, or brooding over how uncomfortable you are right now, simply change your thoughts. That is all that is necessary.

Imagine yourself living in the apartment of your dreams. It does not matter if you don't have enough money right now. Just imagine yourself living in your 'new' apartment and see it as a reality, *focus on it*. It *will* present itself to you soon! When you want something badly enough, the whole universe conspires to give it to you. That's Creative Visualisation.

> *'The future belongs to those who believe in the beauty of their dreams.'*
>
> —Eleanor Roosevelt
> longest serving First Lady of the United States
> during the service term of her husband President
> Franklin D. Roosevelt (1933-1945).

How to use Creative Visualisation

Many people use visualisation techniques to manifest success and fulfilling relationships, to learn to love and heal themselves or others, or to find direction on their spiritual paths. By using your imagination and focusing on your dreams you can create love, peace, success, health and happiness in your life. However, two things need to be kept in mind—first of all, you need to be absolutely sincere about your dream. And secondly, you need to focus entirely, heart and soul, on your dream.

For instance, if you wish to harmonise your relationship with a co-worker or a member of your family you can use Creative Visualisation to bring about the peace you desire. To do this, first you need to obtain a state of deep relaxation. There are a number of meditation techniques that can assist you in this process, the simplest being deep breathing and clearing your mind of all distractions.

Once relaxed, imagine that you are confronting the person you are having problems with and that the two of you are having an open and honest discussion. Imagine that you are feeling waves of love and respect from that person and that you are being loved in return.

Seeing this mental image may be difficult initially but with perseverance you can do it. Some people have realised that they feel anger rather than love towards a person because of past wrongs or ill words. If this is the case, acknowledge the negative emotion but move away from the feeling of anger to a feeling of love. You will be truly amazed with the result.

You may initially find it difficult to focus your mind so intensely on your dream. If so, just relax ... literally! Your conscious mind is busy constantly trying to solve your day-to-day problems and is burdened with preconceived ideas and conditioning. That's why you need to relax and calm your active conscious mind first, before you can focus on your subconscious mind and your dream.

The following exercises will help you clear your mind and create that which you desire:

Be sure you are seated comfortably, with no interruptions, and clear your mind of all thoughts. To assist in the process you may wish to use some meditation techniques by concentrating on breathing slowly and fully for a few minutes. As your mind becomes clear, begin to create your desire by picturing it in your mind. Focus on the important elements within your desire and chant a positive statement that will enhance this process.

For example, if you want to do well in your exams you may use a positive statement like – 'I am smart, I trust my brain and I will score the marks I want', or 'Everything I have read is stored somewhere in my memory and I will be able to recall it when I need it.'

Continue to focus on your desire and repeat your affirmations. Some people will find it difficult initially to remain focused and stop the conscious mind from drifting off. If this occurs, clear your mind of all thoughts and commence your exercise once again.

Focus on your desire for as long as you feel is necessary. This may vary amongst individuals. Creative Visualisation exercises can be practised at any time of the day and do not require you to hold any particular religious beliefs. It only requires you to believe in one thing—your dream.

'Go confidently in the direction of your dreams.
Live the life you've always imagined.'

—Henry David Thoreau
19th century American author,
philosopher, development critic, historian and
leading transcendentalist.

Here's the inspiring story of one man who believed so much in the power of his visions, that his dreams literally took flight!

J.R.D. Tata—the Indian aviator

J.R.D. Tata believed in reaching for the skies, literally. Flying was his passion, and he became India's first licensed pilot in 1929, his license bearing the pioneering number 1!

J.R.D. founded Tata Aviation in 1932, and in August that same year, he spiritedly flew a single-handed De Havilland Puss Moth himself, carrying airmail from Karachi to Bombay (now Mumbai)!

And so Tata Aviation was born, based out of a hut with a thatched roof at Juhu, Bombay, with a staff of just one pilot and two apprentice mechanics and a 'fleet' of only two aircrafts!

After Tata Aviation's initial runs and its conversion into a public limited company with the name Air India, J.R.D. went on to establish Air India International in 1948. Under his vision, this simple airline grew into a state-owned flag carrier, with a fleet of over 100 planes, covering over 75 domestic and international destinations. What a long way to come from a thatched hut base and small fleet of two!

From an extremely humble beginning, J.R.D. Tata built India's first international airline and brought commercial aviation to the country!

J.R.D. Tata was a true pioneer who changed the face of the world. He had a dream and was not afraid to reach out and grasp it. His passion and his dedication helped him create a strong, viable airline from simply two planes and a handful of people! He did not listen to his detractors who told him it could not be done because it had never been done before, he did not listen when people told him it was tomfoolery to expect to build a fleet of aircrafts for an 'airline' which was controlled from a hut. He only listened to the voice inside him that whispered, 'Yes, you can touch the skies, if only you trust yourself, and try!'

'There is no passion to be found playing small—in settling for a life that is less than the one you are capable of living.'

—Nelson Mandela

Remember to dream BIG! Believe in the power of those BIG dreams, and you will live a remarkable life.

Magic Mantra Seven

I HAVE EVERYTHING I WANT IN LIFE

Magic Mantra Seven

I have everything I want in life

Affirmations

> *As a man thinketh in his heart, so is he.*
>
> —Proverbs 23:7 (The Bible)

Affirmations are positive statements we say over and over to ourselves, till they become firmly embedded in our minds. Affirmations repeated over long periods of time actually have the power to change our attitudes, elevate our self-esteem, and even bring our dreams right to our doorsteps!

No kidding!

Emile Coué, the 19th-century French professor and master hypnotist, became a pioneer of affirmation techniques—curing hundreds of patients in Europe and North America by teaching his patients to repeat the following affirmation each morning and evening:

'Every day, in every way, I'm getting better and better.'

Using this affirmation *alone*, the healing results were nothing less than spectacular!

Remember; thoughts produce actions!

Affirmations have long been recognised as powerful tools to manifest desires. That's because the subconscious mind cannot differentiate between actual reality and suggestions. Therefore, it processes what you keep telling it – *affirmations* – as being real, and goes about using its powerful creative ability to actualise those affirmations and turn them into concrete reality! So basically, if you constantly say positive things to yourself, your mind will start believing them and create your world accordingly, giving you success, health, and happiness!

For this reason, people from all walks of life – from athletic coaches to sales professionals, from religious leaders to performance experts – promote the practice of affirmations.

Affirmations are also used to reprogramme negative thoughts with positive ideas. They can be used to completely transform your attitude towards life and make you a happier person!

Affirmations can be used during your visualisation exercise or any other time of the day. You can chant, sing, say them out loud, or simply say them in your mind to yourself.

Use some of the following affirmations to help you create that which you desire:

If you want to feel happier about yourself and your life, you could try saying, 'I love the person I am' or 'My life is wonderful.'

If you feel your confidence needs a boost you could repeat, 'I am capable of achieving everything I desire.'

To feel better about your body or give yourself a figurative shot in the arm when you're feeling unwell, you could try saying, 'I am healthy' or 'I look and feel great!'

To help clear your mind during meditation you could try saying to yourself, 'I am in contact with God and in touch with the divine light' or 'I am now at peace.'

When saying your affirmations, remember to use the words 'I now' or 'I am,' as if it already exists, rather than 'I will' or 'in the future.' This allows the universe to create what you desire now rather than later. Also make sure that your request is one that meets your *immediate* goals.

For example: If you wish to lose weight, say, 'I am thin now.' This allows your body to adjust now to the size and shape you wish to be.

To attract love, you may try any of the following affirmations––'I am a loving and caring person and deserve to have loving people around me,' or 'I am now ready for a lasting and loving relationship and deserve to be happy,' or 'I am surrounded by love and happiness and will continue to attract this.'

Remember to use short and simple affirmations, as these prove far more successful.

Healing visualisations

Creative Visualisation is a powerful tool to create and maintain a state of good health. Your mind is constantly sending messages to your body about the environment you live in, and your state of mind actually has the power to affect your physical body! That's why, when your mind is stressed, you often fall prey to physical illnesses. It's also why sports coaches give their teams 'pep talks' before big games!

If your mind tells your body to react in a certain manner, it will.

I knew a woman in her mid thirties who would literally *shake* in fear every time she approached a swimming pool!

She had no recollection of almost drowning or of any other incident that explained this unnatural fear. Then we stumbled upon an interesting fact: her mother was petrified of water too! We soon realised that her mother had unwittingly passed on her own fear of water to her daughter. And this fear became so embedded in her daughter's mind that now, even though it was irrational, it was enough to make her body react violently whenever she saw a swimming pool!

Our minds often literally *create* illness when we do not want to confront a certain situation, or are extremely tense, or when we need time off from work. Illness is often a direct result of our own thoughts and mental state! So, to put it simply, be cheerful and positive, and you'll feel healthier!

Thoughts produce action!

To improve your health, here are some affirmations you could try—'I am fit and eat healthy food at regular intervals of time,' or 'I eat a lot of fruits and vegetables and feel the difference it has made to my skin and body.' You could feel fitter by repeating, 'I exercise every day and love how healthy I feel!' or 'I am playing tennis (or any other sport) and loving it!'

Visualisations for success

Success can be defined in a lot of ways. To you, success could mean recognition, or wealth, or personal satisfaction, or simply being able to do what you want! It could be *any or all* of these things! The great news is ... whatever your ideal for success may be, if you are able to visualise it, you will definitely be able to achieve it.

Thoughts produce action!

Realise that your lack of success may be related to your own emotions and attitude! Examine what you are feeling and thinking. Are you pessimistic about your chances of succeeding? If you believe that you are destined to fail because you are unlucky or your background is weak; then you *will* fail! To change your world you first must change your beliefs. To make your life amazing, you first must be positive about life!

You may wish to try the following affirmations to attract success–'I enjoy my work,' or 'My job is wonderful and financially rewarding,' or 'I am wealthy now and in a well-paid position,' or 'I can now have *everything* I desire.' You could even try, 'I am appreciated for the good work that I do,' or 'My work is a pleasurable challenge,' or, simply, 'I am terrific at my work!'

Use your imagination to the fullest. Imagine winning awards, or taking exotic vacations you have always dreamed of. Imagine exciting new assignments, or a whopping salary hike from your employer!

Good luck!

At any time during these visualisation exercises, if you realise you're finding it difficult to remain focused, clear your mind of all thoughts and commence your Creative Visualisation again. Continue to focus on your desire for as long as you feel is necessary; there is no fixed time for anyone. You will know for yourself when you feel happiness taking form inside.

Here's an inspiring story about two brothers who dreamt of flying and who worked hard to make their dream a reality!

Flight of the Wrights

You may have heard of Orville and Wilbur Wright, the legendary Wright Brothers. This dynamic duo invented and built the world's first successful aeroplane in 1903! Very soon after that, they developed their flying contraption into the first practical fixed-wing aircraft, and became famous as the first to invent aircraft controls that made fixed-wing powered flight possible! Their invented controls are still the standard for all fixed-wing aircrafts even today, more than a century later!

As children, Orville and Wilbur were both fascinated by the concept of flying. When the brothers were ages seven and 11, their father brought them a toy 'helicopter'. The toy was made of cork, bamboo and paper, with a rubber band to twirl its twin blades, and it was a little bigger than an adult's hand. The Wright brothers played with their toy helicopter till it broke, and then built a new one of their own! The brothers later said this toy initially sparked their interest in flight.

During their early years, Orville, though academically bright, dropped out of high school to start a printing press in 1889, having designed and built his own printing press with Wilbur's help. Wilbur was going through depression after a tragic ice-hockey accident, which resulted in the loss of all his front teeth, and corroded his confidence. However, as the printing press picked up, Wilbur shook off his depression and enthusiastically joined as editor in his brother's print shop.

The next step for the two enterprising brothers was capitalising on the bicycle craze that was spreading across America. They opened up a bicycle repair and sales shop in 1892 and soon they were manufacturing their own brand! They gained the mechanical skills that helped them build their aeroplanes by working for years

in their shop with printing presses, bicycles, motors and other machinery. Their work with bicycles in particular influenced their belief that an unstable vehicle like a flying machine could be controlled and balanced with practice. From 1900 until their first powered flights in late 1903, they conducted extensive glider tests that not only developed their skills as pilots, but also trained them and taught them many aviation techniques.

So how did the Wright Brothers finally succeed? They grabbed every opportunity that came their way, they followed the dreams that captured their minds and proved to the world that they could make them realities! Success did not come instantly, but they learnt invaluable lessons on the way … and these lessons ultimately sealed their triumph. The Wright brothers visualised their sky-high goal with crystal clarity and decided with absolute certainty that they would be the first to succeed at it, and that, in a nutshell, is how they actually did it.

Remember,

> *'Courage doesn't always roar. Sometimes courage is the quiet voice at the end of the day saying, "I will try again tomorrow."'*
>
> —Mary Anne Radmacher
> writer of motivational books, creator of
> inspirational quotes, an artist and a calligrapher.

Magic Mantra Eight

WILL PACE MYSELF AND AVOID BURNOUT!

Magic Mantra Eight

I will pace myself and avoid burnout!

Balance your life

> *Life is not measured by the number of breaths we take, but by the moments that take our breath away.*
>
> —Maya Angelou
> American author and poet, credited with plays, movies and television shows spanning more than fifty years.

There are certain times in our lives when we feel stretched to our limits. Usually this is when we have over-committed ourselves, emotionally, financially, or even with our time. This obsessive drive to do *everything* at the same time can lead to tension, fatigue, and ultimately, burnout.

What is burnout?

Burnout is a popular term to describe the condition of exhaustion and frustration commonly associated with over-achievers. In their race to achieve unrealistic goals, these over-achievers just don't know when to stop; and they wind up depleting their energy thoroughly and ruining their mental and physical health. Ironically, it is usually people who have been most energetic and enthusiastic about their work who run the greatest risk of burnout. The enthusiasm they exhibited at the beginning of a project gradually recedes as expectations of success or achievement fade. The person then becomes listless, impatient, physically exhausted, and tends to lose all interest.

There are several warning signs of the onset of burnout. The failure to set priorities when faced with alternative and conflicting areas of responsibility is one. Another danger is when the person is left without a clear indication of his or her role. With no guidelines, they will feel that they have failed to achieve what was expected of them. Frequently, the problem is associated with the individual's own willingness to take on too much responsibility. Burnout arises when they finally have taken up more than can be handled by one person.

Another reliable warning sign of the advent of burnout is over-defensiveness. When you are juggling many tasks and success means everything to you, you will react badly to criticism. So take a moment here to think about how defensive you actually are.

It is a common trait for ambitious people to repackage blunders so they don't look so bad. It is also very easy to blame circumstances, luck or others when things don't work out. But these reactions often don't solve the situation at all! Most people can tell what you're up to, and it would be far simpler and much more impressive to just face the situation, accept your mistake and strive to improve. It won't help you to argue back forcefully, or blame someone else or even feel hurt and withdrawn. And it certainly won't help to get angry and vow to get even!

Being less defensive and more teachable is a healthy way to deal with stress and will prevent burnout!

Remember, a little defensiveness is healthy self-protection—like your immune system. However, excessive defensiveness creates negativity and can even prevent you from learning through your mistakes! So be open to suggestions and making improvements; it's all part of the learning process!

There are times when you will feel angry because of changes imposed from above. You may resent this and try to make yourself feel better by commenting on the 'stupidity' of your boss or teacher. But this move can be self-defeating if it stops you from understanding his or her rationale. After all, they probably have more experience than you, so it may not be a bad idea to try to understand where they're coming from!

If you have healthy self-esteem, you should be able to admit your mistakes! It's when you have low self-esteem that you will either beat yourself up over the smallest of mistakes OR go to the other extreme and defensively never admit them!

You may share your negative emotions with your friends by telling them a certain project will fail even before you begin it! What you're doing is actually setting up your defences in advance so you won't have to create them later. Advance defensiveness can actually *increase* the likelihood of failure! Some people will even sabotage their own projects, when they start to think they will fail, if they can do so in a way that ensures their getting off the hook. Recognising and avoiding your own excessive defensiveness is not easy if you have developed a pattern of protecting a fragile self esteem this way. But you will not be able to keep up with the fast-paced learning required in today's organisations, if you don't confront this issue for yourself.

Steps to counter burnout

There are some clear and effective steps to be taken when the signs of burnout appear. The onset of fatigue and inability to relax needs to be explored. Have you always felt under pressure to succeed? If not, try to recall when this driving force first became over-important to you.

Can you identify a period when you started to lose your sense of humour? Can you recall when you first started having disagreements with your friends and colleagues? Was there a time when your responsibilities became a matter of overpowering personal involvement, when you were identifying with them to the extent that *you measured your own personal success or failure with that of the work you were doing?*

If the answer to even some of these questions is 'yes', it is a clear indication that it is time to re-evaluate your values and priorities. When work is no longer a pleasurable challenge, it is time to consider what changes need to be made. Do you need to change your priorities? Do you need to change your duties? Do you need to change your job? Or do you simply need a break?

If you're going through burnout, there are no prescriptions that anyone else can provide to deal with it better than those you can provide yourself, *once you allow yourself to become aware of your needs*! It is your own wellbeing that is at stake, and it has to be your own choice to fix your life. You now need to get in touch with yourself, with your values and what you ultimately want out of your life. You need to decide that, at the end of the day, would you rather be at the end of your tether, or look forward to a bright new day? Silly question! But how many people, I wonder, suffering the symptoms of burnout, take time out to ask themselves that silly question?

It's now time to sit down and actually make a list of typical external factors that stress you out. Put them in descending order; from the most frustrating to the least stressful and see which of these factors you can actually change. Write down exactly what creates that feeling of tension inside you. Is it because you cannot say no to these things often enough? Or is it because you have not prioritised your jobs? Some people are perfectionists and are their own greatest taskmasters. Are you a perfectionist who is driving himself crazy? If so, learn to relax and not be so hard on yourself. Learn to appreciate the good work you have done by rewarding yourself with something fun and relaxing. This will not only give you peace but also refresh and energise you to take on your next goal!

You also need to understand that you cannot always control external events but you CAN control how you react to them. Your first step should be to realise that no person or external event can **make** you feel anything. Try and change your reaction to things—laugh more, distance yourself, lighten up a little and try to maintain a better balance between your work and your personal life.

Remember the words of Danny Kaye, 'Life is a great big canvas, and you should throw all the paint on it you can!'

The following suggestions may help you deal with your anxiety better:

It is important to remember that we *all* feel anxious about some things—it's only human! If others don't seem so tense, it's probably only because they have learnt to hide it better!

If you're feeling stressed, it may help to write down all the negative things you say to yourself. And whenever you catch yourself doing this, just write down the opposite point of view! You'll see the positive slant is just a different way of looking at the same facts! Anxiety often creates a distorted view of things, which creates more anxiety! And the best way to eliminate distortion is by checking your view with others—so give yourself a reality check! Start talking about your anxiety in small ways; you may often find that others are experiencing a similar problem! This makes it easier to open up fully and gives you a healthier perspective of your problems.

Then it's simply a matter of breaking your anxiety down into specifics that you can knock off one at a time. Keeping it all in your head seems overwhelming, so *write it down*. Examine the external factors that make you tense and change whatever can be changed. For the rest, work on changing how you react to pressure! Strive to improve your self-esteem and try relaxation techniques to help you feel calmer and more confident.

Relaxation exercises

There are a number of techniques you can use to attain a relaxed state. These can be used at any time of the day or night.

Ensure you are seated comfortably with no interruptions and clear your mind of all thoughts. You may wish to use some meditation techniques and concentrate on breathing slowly and fully for a few minutes. As your mind becomes clear, imagine that all the physical stress in your body is being removed. During your exhales of deep breath, imagine the stress and tension being expelled from your body and disintegrating into the air. As you visualise the stress leaving your body, you will begin to feel more relaxed. Focus on this relaxed state and say an affirmation that will enhance this process. You could use any of the following statements—'I am in a totally relaxed state,' 'My mind is clear and my body has released all its stress and tension,' or 'I am protected from harm and feel great.' You could even try repeating, 'I am relaxed and at peace,' 'I feel inner peace and tranquility,' or simply, 'I feel serene.'

If you find it difficult to remain focused, clear your mind of all thoughts and commence your Creative Visualisation again, for as long as it takes you to feel completely relaxed.

Leading a balanced life

Many people believe that schools and corporations love people who are obsessed with achievement and are willing to take on any number of tasks at any time. They take these as signs of ambition and dedication. But that's not true; burnout is an unhealthy sign of someone who simply cannot manage his or her time!

N.R. Narayana Murthy, highly successful industrialist, software engineer, and Founder and Chairman Emeritus of Infosys Technologies Ltd., is himself a great believer in leading a balanced life, as is evident from the story below.

N.R. Narayana Murthy has worked very hard to reach where he is today. He founded Infosys in 1981, simply on a vision he believed in, and Rs 1000 borrowed from his wife!

After putting up the initial capital for Infosys, Murthy invited six other professional engineers to join him. He then worked dedicatedly as CEO of Infosys for 21 years, building Infosys to what it is today—a software giant with a cool turnover of US dollars 6.041 billion! Certainly a long way from the Rs 1000 it was founded with!

The path to greatness is never easy. It is riddled with challenges that demand hard work, commitment and a passion to succeed. In today's time, it seems almost impossible to even survive without pushing harder, or faster, or *longer* than everyone else. Narayana Murthy has been through the super-competitive grind and has emerged a winner and few would know the value of hard work better than he. But even fewer know the difference between hard working and smart working. Therein lies the real kernel of wisdom. So read this speech given by Mr Narayana Murthy and see if it makes sense in your hectic, jumbled, life-is-a-race, lifestyle.

Why should we go home on time?
(Speech delivered by industrialist N.R. Narayana Murthy at a Mentorship Programme)

'I know people who work 12 hours a day, six days a week, or more. Some people do so because of a work emergency where the long hours are only temporary. Other people I know have put in these hours for years.

'I do not know if they are working all these hours, but I do know they are in the office this long. Others put in long office hours because they are addicted to the workplace.

'Whatever the reason for putting in overtime, working long hours over the long term is harmful to the person and to the organisation. There are things managers can do to change this for everyone's benefit. Being in the office long hours, over long periods of time, makes way for potential errors.

'My colleagues who are in the office for long hours, frequently make mistakes caused by fatigue. Correcting these mistakes requires their time as well as the time and energy of others. I have seen people work Tuesday through Friday to correct mistakes made after 5:00 pm on Monday.

'Another problem is that people who are in the office for long hours are not pleasant company. They often complain about other people (who are not working as hard); they are irritable, or cranky, or even angry. Other people avoid them. Such behaviour poses problems, where work goes much better when people work together instead of avoiding one another.

'Suggestions to put some balance in their lives can be:

1) Wake up, eat a good breakfast and go to work.
2) Work hard and smart for eight or nine hours.
3) Go home.
4) Read books/comics, watch a funny movie, dig in the dirt, play with your kids, etc.
5) Eat well and sleep well.

'This is called *recreating*. Doing steps 1, 3, 4, and 5 enable step 2.

'Working regular hours and recreating daily are simple concepts. They are hard for some of us because that requires a 'personal change.' They are possible since we all have the power to choose to do them.

'Perhaps some people put in such long hours because they do not want to miss anything when they leave the office. The trouble with this is that events will never stop happening. That is life! Things happen 24 hours a day.

'Allowing for so little rest is not ultimately practical. So, take a nap. Things will happen while you are asleep, but you will have the energy to catch up when you're awake.'

Narayana Murthy's words are hitting home in today's crazy, maddening lifestyle, and are not applicable only to office working cultures. They apply to the way we live our lives at all stages and ages – the way we want to attend those million tuitions, buy all the reference books we will beat ourselves up over never reading, stay up worrying about that one extra mark – and forgetting that there is another side of life altogether.

So, do not burn yourself up to live life. Enjoy it, work harder than ever and give yourself a pat on the back, but know when to stop, know when to give your body and mind a break, and everything else will simply fall into place more beautifully than before. Studies can be tormenting, peer pressure can be tough to fight, competition can be nerve-wracking and fear of failure almost paralysing, but *none* of these is worth losing your health over.

Remember that there is a time and place for everything, including fun, late nights, and studies—they enhance each other in tandem. But there is no point in stretching yourself so tautly over everything you *must* accomplish that you break without ever appreciating the beauty of life that lies in keeping it all balanced.

After all, in the words of the great philosopher Seneca, 'When shall we live, if not now?'

Magic Mantra Nine

I CAN COPE WITH MY PROBLEMS

Magic Mantra Nine

I can cope with my problems

Coping with tough times and helping others cope

> *All the adversity I've had in my life; all my troubles and obstacles have strengthened me.*
>
> —Walt Disney

Destiny deals different cards to everyone, and each person has a unique life. Some may seem lucky, while others are not. The bottom line is, playing a good game out of the cards in *your* hand!

Coping with the cards life has dealt you

Things like the death of a parent; alcoholism in the family that afflicts either of a parent or a sibling; drug abuse; financial constraints; discord between parents; or legal wrangling beyond the nuclear family are all terrible issues that unfortunately need to be coped with.

Alcoholism, for example, has reared its ugly head even among teenagers today. Lax rules, corruption, and closed lines of communication between teenagers and parents have led to an increasing number of teenage drug and alcohol abuse issues. In fact, several alcohol companies market fruit-flavoured alcoholic drinks as 'mild alcohols', hooking young teenagers at an early age. These adolescent addictions flare out into major problems as one grows older and gains more responsibility.

If you realise that you have a problem and need help, or if you know someone who does, the Alcoholics' Anonymous and other such anonymous organisations working with alcoholics and counselling them are wonderfully supportive organisations that have succeeded in rehabilitating thousands of troubled people. These groups provide a very strong support system and circle of friends to help alcoholics. Reformed alcoholics usually admit that their excessive alcohol consumption was triggered off by low self-esteem. So having good friends or a supportive member of your family around would raise your self-esteem and automatically reduce your need for alcohol.

You need to realise that you don't need alcohol or drugs to feel happy. Your life is a precious and beautiful gift, which you must appreciate. And your life will offer you enough, and more, to delight in and amaze you, always.

Alcoholism is in fact, just *one* version of obsessive-compulsive behaviour. Obsessions can be anything; you will find people who are hooked onto drugs, socialising, eating, exercising power, or even working! In fact I was told by a reformed alcoholic that if you substitute the word 'alcoholic' with another synonymous word like workaholic or even 'peopleholic' you will find that the symptoms are very similar! It is difficult to cope with these addictions and it is only by resorting to counselling help, or talking about it to a close friend or family member, or joining support groups, that success can be achieved. But you need to take that first step and regain control over your life.

Coping with the death of a loved one

While you are in school or college, you may have to face the unfortunate tragedy of losing a loved one, whether a grandparent or parent. Usually, facing death as a young person is very difficult because one is not only grieving over the actual separation and terrible sense of loss, but also because the concept of death is difficult to handle.

The initial reaction is usually shock and denial. It often takes two to three weeks to believe the news when you first hear it. You have to be gentle on yourself and allow yourself to feel all the emotions that threaten to overwhelm you. Grief is emotionally, mentally, and physically, very draining, and you may feel more pain than you ever believed possible. It is extremely important at this stage to let yourself experience your pain and sorrow and not try to 'be strong' for others. We cannot 'get around' grief; we must 'go through' it in order to accept the reality of the loss of our loved one and be able to move on.

Aftershocks and reorganisation

In this stage, you ultimately reach the point where you have conquered your grief and its grip on you. You eventually gain the ability to think of your lost loved one without heart-wrenching pain. There will always be a sense of sadness, but it will no longer be that terrible, drowning grief. Developing a relationship of memory with your lost loved one is helpful and rewarding. One way to memorialise your loved one is to withdraw emotional energy from grieving and reinvest that energy productively in other activities. You must realise that your loved one would want you to be happy. Just as we know that loss is inevitable, we know that recovering from sorrow can in fact also be inevitable, as unlikely as it may seem.

> *'What is extraordinary about us is that we each have the capacity to rise like a phoenix out of our ashes, to create ourselves newly, to begin again. We can transform ourselves and our lives, regardless of what we have*

> *endured before. Maybe the true purpose of suffering is that out of our pain, we will rise, expand, grow and achieve.'*
>
> —Judy Tatelbaum
> licensed clinical social worker,
> psychotherapist and inspirational speaker.

Judy Tatelbaum suggests we use our loss as a loving testimonial to the deceased, by reaching out and helping others. We could participate in, or lead support groups (big or small, formal or informal) to help others deal with their tragic experiences, or simply to prevent others from going through what we have gone through ourselves.

Unconditional support is the greatest gift we can give to the bereaved. Just being there to provide a hand to hold, a shoulder to cry on, a sympathetic ear, or just your quiet presence and unconditional love may truly help someone out of their darkness.

Remember, just when you think you have nothing left to give others, you reach into your heart and find something more.

> *'The best and most beautiful things in the world cannot be seen or even touched—they must be felt with the heart.'*
>
> —Helen Keller
> sight and hearing impaired speaker and political activist; passionate advocate for the working class, women's rights and people with disabilities.

The light within—the story of Helen Keller

When Helen Keller was a baby, only 19 months old, a severe illness destroyed her vital senses of sight and hearing. This restricted her communication to only rough signals and unintelligible sounds, as she had no idea how to talk, or even identify things in the world around her. Imagine not knowing what even the simplest things you touch are called. Imagine not having a word, or a name for anything around you. Imagine the frustration that would build up in a curious mind with no way to express itself. That was Helen's darkness *every single day*.

But the human mind is an amazing thing that always finds a way to reach out and grow. By the age of seven, the precocious Helen already had over 60 signs she used, to communicate with her family! Unfortunately, she was still unable to communicate with the outside world at all.

Then, in 1887, when Helen was seven years old, Anna Sullivan arrived at the Keller household. Anna herself was visually impaired and only 20 years old, but she had a clear idea of the nurturing Helen would need. She immediately began teaching Helen to communicate by spelling words into her palm, beginning with the word 'd-o-l-l', a gift she had brought for Helen. Until now, Helen did not understand that every object had a word uniquely identifying it, and at first, it seemed like an overwhelming concept to swallow. In fact, Helen got so frustrated when Anna was trying to teach her the word for 'mug' that she even broke the doll in a fit of rage!

Helen's progress through education was slow and painful, but her breakthrough was just as beautiful. This breakthrough came when she felt cool water run over one of her hands, and suddenly realised that the motions Anna was making on her other palm **symbolised the idea of 'water'**. In a flash, Helen was swept away in a torrent of words and their meanings flooding her mind, and she fell in love with the beauty and power of words. Little Helen was suddenly ravenous to learn more and more, and delighted Anna Sullivan with her insatiable appetite for knowledge and literature.

Later in her life, Helen Keller described how knowledge always transformed her life and thoughts, famously saying, 'Knowledge is love and light and *vision*.'

Knowledge was dawn breaking over Helen's world of darkness.

Helen was so enamoured by the knowledge that had lit up her life, that she went on to study at Radcliffe University and became the first hearing and vision impaired person to earn a Bachelor of Arts degree!

Helen also wrote passionately, becoming a prolific writer with over 12 published books, her first being at age 11! At age 22 she published her most famous book, her autobiography, titled *The Story of My Life*, which is revered all over the world as a source of inspiration and motivation.

Helen also emerged as a world-famous speaker and political activist. She advocated passionately for the working class, women's rights, people with disabilities and many other causes. She travelled the world extensively and met with many prominent figures, including presidents, scientists, and influential writers.

Helen did not restrain herself from following her dreams because she felt sorry for herself, she did not feel disheartened because she was not born as lucky as others; she got up and tried to make the world a better place, saying, 'I am only one, but still I am one. I cannot do everything, but still I can do something; and because I cannot do everything, I will not refuse to do something that I *can* do.'

Helen Keller did not let her tragic problems become her disabilities; she *used her understanding* of physical disabilities instead to reach out to those in need of help!

So take inspiration from this story of a strong woman, who fought overwhelming odds every day, but who did not let even her lack of sight and hearing dull the joy and beauty she saw in life. Do not crumble under the weight of one challenge, one disappointment, one tragedy, or one failure; however large and monstrous it may seem. When everything around you seems wrong and twisted, and you feel all alone in your darkness, remember Helen Keller—a woman who emerged from complete darkness and reached out to make the world a more beautiful place.

> *'All the world is full of suffering ... It is also full of overcoming.'*
>
> —Helen Keller

Magic Mantra Ten

I WILL ENRICH MY EMOTIONAL LIFE

Magic Mantra Ten

I will enrich my emotional life

Discovering new emotions and relationships

> *It is confidence in our bodies, minds and spirits that allows us to keep looking for new adventures, new directions to grow in, and new lessons to learn—which is what life is all about.*
>
> —Oprah Winfrey

Adolescence is a wonderful, exciting time because it is the time when you forge new friendships—relationships that will probably last a lifetime and will play a large role in the decisions you make. Good friends who accept and like you for the way you are, who don't use you, who are honest with you and support you, will make your life wonderful. Bad friends, who make you miserable, or lie or abuse you, or lead you into dangerous waters, can ruin your life. It's important to choose your friends carefully, as they will be a great influence on your self-esteem and on how you spend your free time.

Adolescence is also the period when you first venture out to have an adult relationship. You begin to specially notice not only the opposite sex but also other types of people who never interested you before. This is the time when you fall in love. Sometimes it's just a crush and you notice your heart beating faster or louder when that special someone walks into the room or smiles at you. Very often you discuss the object of your affection with your friends to see if you made the right choice, and sometimes your friends' opinions don't even matter. Unfortunately, very often when people fall in love for the first time it is with someone completely *unsuitable*. The trick is to take it easy and not rush headlong into a tangled relationship that makes you feel miserable or hampers your growth or destroys all your other relationships with your family or friends. Remember the time will come when you will meet that special person who will love you for who you are; who will respect you and not try to control you, and who will share beautiful moments with you and make you happy! You do not have to settle for anything less, trust me. You deserve all that you have dreamed of!

It is so important that you learn to know and love **yourself** first and appreciate **your own talents** before entering into a relationship. Today's youngsters are getting into relationships very early and often before they discover even basic things about themselves—what they would like to do with their lives, what they wish to study or even what kind of person they want to be!

> *'To say "I love you" one must first know how to say the "I"'*
>
> —Howard Roark in Ayn Rand's *The Fountainhead*.

Whatever may your age be, whatever the period in your life, never put up with abuse – physical or mental – in a relationship. Respect yourself more than that. If the person you are with is overly possessive, jealous, controlling, physically violent, manipulative, or just makes you miserable constantly, it may be time to take a deep breath and get out. It will work out best for both of you. Relationships like these will one day have a bitter ending for *at least* one of the people involved.

Remember, love should never feel bad. If something doesn't feel right, listen to yourself, listen to your feelings, listen to your heart and *do something about it*! You have to teach the other person, with love, understanding, and respect, how you should be treated and what you want and need from a special friend. And if there is not the slightest of efforts or care to even *try* to make you happy, let go of the relationship. You deserve better.

I'm not saying relationships are easy. Relationships can be pretty difficult; we have to make an effort to work at them. But the important things are: **good communication, patience, respect, kindness and honesty**. We have to learn to express our feelings without hurting others; to be honest without insulting; to respect other people's opinions and beliefs and to try and make them understand how we feel without putting them down, demeaning them, or blaming them. Once we insult someone, it will be hard for that person to trust us, no matter how many times we apologise.

And, of course, **we have to learn to forgive**. We all make mistakes and want others to forgive us for our faults and weaknesses. If we hurt someone's feelings, we should say 'I'm sorry' and mean it! If our actions or words hurt the feelings of people we love and appreciate – even if we didn't mean to hurt them – we **should** apologise and let the other person know that we truly care. It should be a sincere apology or it will mean nothing and trust will die.

We will all make many mistakes in our relationships, but hopefully we will learn our lessons and try to change. And yes, we have the power to change; we can learn to act in different ways, we can learn to control our anger, to become more loving and affectionate, to show more concern, to be more understanding and to pay more attention. We can definitely learn to be more compassionate and kind; more patient and tolerant! The difference we see in how others respond to us will be our greatest reward!

Love is not easy—but the challenge is worth it!

Remember, these principles you're reading about are applicable to *all* relationships—with parents, grandparents, siblings, boyfriend or girlfriend, friends, or even teachers or colleagues! The foundation of *all* relationships boils down to the same thing—respect, love, acceptance, and honesty.

The hardest thing is to love without expectations, without conditions, without judgements; learning to express your feelings but respecting how your boyfriend/girlfriend, husband/wife, parents, siblings, or friend feels; to let the loved ones be free; free to be themselves, free to grow, free to accomplish his/her goals and dreams! It's the hardest thing to do, but you can do it!

Remember, your thoughts are the source of virtually everything in your life. If your relationship is lousy, it's because you think of it that way. The person you're in a relationship with isn't with you every moment, but your thoughts about that person are. If you change your thoughts to what you love about that person from what you've always labelled as wrong, you've just changed your entire relationship! **It went from lousy to great just by changing your mind!**

Be positive! You need to concentrate on others' good qualities and appreciate their efforts to make you happy. Do not expect so much that you will never be satisfied or pleased with anything they do.

'Turn your face to the sun and the shadows fall behind you.'
—Maori proverb

Be honest with the people you love. Trust can take a relationship through its worst storms and mistrust can rock even the steadiest of relationships. When we lie, cheat, gossip, or steal, we cause *mistrust;* once people have a reason to doubt us, it is very difficult to earn their trust again. We have to work very hard, compromise, and make a firm commitment not to act irresponsibly again to prove that we actually mean what we say.

If you care about someone but you don't love that person, tell him or her, the truth. It will be difficult; but lying at this stage will cause both of you a lot of pain later on. You show due respect to the other person by being honest.

Compromise plays a huge role in most relationships. The particular method a person follows to strike a compromise says much about the kind of relationship the two people involved have worked out together. Meeting someone halfway does involve giving in, although too often we hesitate because we look upon it as giving up. A good compromise is one of the simplest ways to affirm and grow in the love and mutual respect that is so vital to any lasting relationship. Out of true compromise comes *acceptance*. You can never get along perfectly with anyone all the time! In all of your relationships, if you can love someone enough to allow them to be exactly what they choose to be, you will surely achieve peace in your lifetime. True love means you love people for what they are and not for what you think they **should be**.

> *'The primary joy of life is acceptance, approval, the sense of appreciation and companionship of our human comrades. When we are accepted, approved and needed by those who know all about us and like us anyway, we have the first inkling of the peace that transcends understanding.'*
>
> —Joshua Loth Liebman
>
> American rabbi and best-selling author, best known for his book *Peace of Mind*.

Love is a choice. Happiness is a choice. Patience is a choice. Peace is a choice.

Consider this scenario:

You meet a wonderfully exciting person and you are initially thrilled by that person's attention and possessiveness. You believe that the more possessive the person is, the more he/she loves and needs you. It seems to be heady and exciting for you—being so desired by another person!

Yet at the same time your partner, who claims to love you so much, often 'puts you down' in public. Then suddenly you find that your partner does not seem to value your opinion or feelings. When you want to do something special, your partner is unavailable, but will later demand all of your time and attention. You begin to feel isolated from your friends and family, so that when your partner isn't there for you, you feel completely alone. When you express unhappiness, you are told, 'This is just the way I am, and if you love me you will understand and accept it.'

Think carefully and answer the question: Is this a mild form of being bullied, or is this just a normal personality difference for which people must make allowances?
Most people would just convince themselves that they need to accept this kind of behaviour, 'love and understand it' and just go on with their lives. But we are learning that this may be a form of **bullying** which may have serious repercussions later on. Most of us are able to recognise the obvious signs of bullying, such as physical violence; but there are more subtle forms of bullying which can be just as damaging, such as verbal and emotional abuse.

Most people continue to believe that it is their own fault that they are being bullied! They are convinced that their actions are provoking the bully and could be controlled, if only they were smarter, richer, socially more acceptable, or better looking! So the first thing to realise is that if you are in a relationship with a bully it is *not* your fault! There is no justification for bullying another person, whether physically, sexually, emotionally, or verbally. There is no way you 'deserve it'!

So, if you find yourself with a bully and you feel helpless, especially when your friend or partner assumes full control over the relationship and attacks your competence continuously, the relationship is not healthy. Does he or she make all the decisions and, further, ridicules or criticises you in public and in private? Are derogatory words like '*stupid*', '*ignorant*'' or '*incompetent*' constantly being flung at you? Do you often feel trapped or on edge? Very often, your bully of a partner will offer no reassurance, stability, or commitment. It will be impossible to predict either his behaviour or his feelings which are 'off-again, on-again.' Frustration results when he fails to satisfy your need for affection, intimacy, attention, acceptance, approval, reassurance, or praise. No matter how hard you try to please him, it is never enough. You will constantly feel rejected and will always be guessing what you did wrong. You will not be able to understand or communicate with your partner and will often feel intimidated by his looks, words or gestures. He will praise others but never mention your achievements; he will 'work the room' but leave you standing alone in the corner. He will use threats of suicide or breaking the relationship as a threat to convince you to accept his behaviour.

Another warning signal of being in a relationship with a bully is an erosion of self-esteem. This would include feelings of diminished self-worth, inadequacy, negative self-image, reduced self-confidence and deterioration of self-respect, with associated depression. Loss of self-esteem happens through a cycle of faulty logic. First, you recognise that you are in a relationship in which you feel unloved, unworthy and mistreated. That you would choose such a relationship causes you to doubt your judgement. You try to 'fix' it by changing yourself or your partner, but when that doesn't work you conclude that you not only have poor judgement, you also are inept at relationship skills.

Thus you reason that 'people get what they deserve,' and since you are being treated badly, you must deserve it. Obviously, the only thing for you to do is to accept the treatment since you 'don't deserve nor could hope for a better relationship.' Hopelessness usually results after numerous failed attempts to communicate the need for a change, with the bullying partner ignoring you entirely. A person who recognises a lack of responsiveness in his/her partner can be warned from the beginning that the relationship is developing in an unhealthy manner, and that there is likely to be trouble ahead.

When the partner who is being bullied responds in kind to the bullying behaviour openly, the result will be hostility characterised by raised voices, hurtful or angry words and accusations against each other. Private hostility includes feelings like hidden resentment, plotted revenge and private negative fantasies. The hostility may also be internalised as guilt or anger.

If you feel that several of the above statements are true of your relationship, you must realise that you need guidance **now**. You need to improve your self-esteem **now**. You could read self-help books, or join a support group or even take the help of family, friends, or teachers. Or you could simply do something that you're good at on your own and take pride in it! Take control over your thoughts and raise your self-esteem to a healthy level. With a realistic self-image and healthy self-esteem you will not allow yourself to be treated so badly.

Here are some suggestions for affirmations to improve your self-esteem. Read them for five whole minutes every morning, and **believe** them—'I am loving'; 'I deserve all that I desire from life'; 'I deserve the best life has to offer'; 'I am attractive'; 'I am well loved by my friends and family'; 'I am talented'; and 'I deserve to be loved and made happy.'

Love yourself, believe in yourself, and know that you **deserve** everything good in life, and nothing less.

As English author Somerset Maugham said, 'It's a funny thing about life; if you refuse to accept anything but the best, you very often get it.'

Conclusion

We all feel that we would be happy and completely satisfied once we have a good job, pleasant relationships, good health, and a comfortable financial condition. We feel that we will finally be at peace when there is nothing to worry about and no need to hurry. Unfortunately life is hardly ever like that! There is *always* something that causes tension or fear.

Often, the moment you think that you are finally in complete control of your life, it suddenly swerves off-course! Situations change, circumstances differ, and people around you move on! Now what do you do? First of all, you need to remember that it is this very vibrant and unpredictable nature of life that gives us joy and our sense of achievement. It allows us to appreciate love and happiness and that keeps all of us so alive.

That being said, in the midst of this vast and often turbulent ocean of life, we do have to learn to cope with our given environment, endeavour to make our planet and our immediate surroundings a little better, and most importantly, strive for a little peace of mind! By 'peace of mind,' I refer to an inner state, independent of your external environment.

Do not forever wait for external circumstances to be 'right' to achieve inner peace. Inner peace is within everybody's reach, independent of outer conditions, wealth or poverty, health or sickness, physical freedom, or the lack of it. Inner peace is independent of even your age or experience! Gone are the days when you had to seek a special mountain peak in the Himalayas and meditate.

Everyone possesses the potential to enjoy peace of mind; all you have to do is tap the peace that already resides inside you!

Throughout every waking moment, thoughts arise in us and dominate our mind. We may choose to ignore them and experience real inner freedom, or we may choose to magnify them with the power of our attention and make them grow.

However, most people forget that they have this choice and are *enslaved* by their thoughts. From the moment they wake up in the morning to the moment they fall asleep at night, the chatter of the mind continues incessantly. The habit of constant, worrisome thinking is very deeply ingrained in the human race. Yet this habit can be undone; **you can choose** the thoughts you wish to allow into your mind!

So choose only positive, happy and uplifting thoughts! Imagine only what you really and truly desire. Remember that your life will be shaped according to your thoughts and that if you smile at the world, the world will smile back at you! Remember that it is *you*r choice; no one is going to tell you how to think or react to situations. The only thing that you really possess in this life is your thoughts. They truly belong to you and you alone, so treasure them.

True control of the mind is not just the ability to concentrate on one thought and disregard other thoughts. It is the ability to cleanse the mind completely and make it silent. I do not mean to tell you that you have to stop using your mind; you *need* to use your mind in order to carry on with your life. I am simply saying that you should learn to control your mind, not the other way around. Your mind is your servant to make your life better; you are the master!

Try to watch your thoughts during the day, as if they are not yours, without being sucked into them. **Become conscious of the fact that you are watching your thoughts**. You will have to remind yourself incessantly to practice watching your thoughts. Do not give up and you will finally succeed. It may take some time but the effort is more than worthwhile. Whenever you find a negative thought preying on your mind, force your mind to look in another direction and train it to become positive.

Remember, whatever new skill we develop, we have to work at it until it turns into second nature, and becomes easy to perform. It's the same with controlling the mind.

These magic mantras have been put together in this little book to show you that you are the master of your own life and destiny. Please choose the mantras you need at the particular stage of life you're at, read the chapter, and see how the suggestions can benefit you! I hope that after reading the anecdotes and stories you will find these magic mantras helpful as you journey towards happiness, love, success, and peace.

I honestly believe you will find and unlock the true potential hidden inside you. I hope that when you make the choices in your life, you will follow your passion, believe in the wonderful person you are and live the life of your dreams.

I wish you all the very best that life has to offer.

Good luck!

Thank you

Many of the thoughts and ideas in this book originated whilst conducting workshops with Haresh Panjabi, who is no longer with us. He invited me to join his organisation 'Life is beautiful' and we conducted various workshops in schools in Mumbai and Nagpur.

Thank you Rosalyn D' Mello for your suggestions and inputs. Svani Parekh and Jennifer Alfonso for your suggestions. Vinayak Pendurkar's illustrations are a delight and I am always happy to work with him.

Laxmi Dhaul
October 2013